'Let me go!'

'Why should I?' A part of my inherita

'You are talking in riddles again,' Claudie protested, but strange fires had ignited inside her, searing through the remnants of her resistance. Desperately, she said, 'Please listen to me!'

Armand sighed and Claudie felt the movement of his breath, a warm current of excitement, through her own body.

'I am listening, *chérie*. To your heart...which doesn't lie.'

Dear Reader

Summer is here at last . . .! And what better way to enjoy these long, long days and warm romantic evenings than in the company of a gorgeous Mills & Boon hero? Even if you can't jet away to an unknown destination with the man of your dreams, our authors can take you there through the power of their storytelling. So pour yourself a long, cool drink, relax, and let your imagination take flight . . .

The Editor

Shirley Kemp was born in South Wales, but has the blood of all four countries of the United Kingdom in her veins. That fact probably explains her infuriatingly impulsive and restless personality, which has recently taken her off to live in France. Second eldest in a family of seven children, she found that spare time was rare, but she read voraciously and wrote for enjoyment. Writing romantic fiction is a natural extension of that youthful pursuit and she still enjoys it just as much.

Recent titles by the same author:

WHEN STRANGERS MEET

INHERITANCE

BY

SHIRLEY KEMP

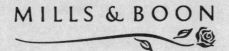

MILLS & BOON

MILLS & BOON LIMITED
ETON HOUSE, 18-24 PARADISE ROAD
RICHMOND, SURREY TW9 1SR

*MILLS & BOON and the Rose Device
are trademarks of the publisher.*

*First published in Great Britain 1994
by Mills & Boon Limited*

© Shirley Kemp 1994

*Australian copyright 1994   Philippine copyright 1994
This edition 1994*

ISBN 0 263 78584 X

*Set in Times Roman 10 on 11½ pt.
01-9408-53394 C*

Made and printed in Great Britain

CHAPTER ONE

CLAUDIE DREW stepped out of the little station into the
brilliance of a June day. It was hot, and tendrils of her
long blonde hair clung damply to her slender neck. She
longed to brush it out and pin it up properly, but that
would have to wait.

The sunlight was dazzling and she rummaged in her
bag for her sunglasses, perching them on her small,
straight nose before looking about a little anxiously.
Someone was supposed to be meeting her here, but the
small car park was deserted.

The people who had got off at the same stop seemed
to have vanished into thin air, making her feel like the
only person in a strangely empty world.

There were some benches along the peach-coloured
wall and she trudged across with her luggage to sit down
on the nearest one.

The train, which had brought her down to this little
town in the South of France, had been surprisingly fast
and clean, but the journey, beginning in London, had
been a long one and fatigue and hunger were beginning
to set in. She'd eaten little. The pâté sandwich she'd ordered from the buffet had turned out to be practically
a whole stick of French bread, crammed with pâté and
pungent slices of garlic. Picking out the pieces had been
like shutting the stable door after the horse had bolted;
the pâté reeked of it. Not wanting to arrive with her
breath aromatic, she'd finally given up.

Not that Armand Delacroix would notice, she mused.
If he was a typical Frenchman, he probably ate the stuff

at every meal. She leaned her head back against the stone wall and closed her eyes, trying to picture him in her mind's eye. It was a game she'd played often over the years, but the vision was never complete. The information her French godmother, Annelise Delacroix, had given her had been too meagre.

Claudie amused herself now, imagining him as the stereotype: short and swarthy and smelling of garlic. It helped keep the anxiety at bay.

Though why she should feel anxious, she didn't know. It wasn't her fault Annelise had left her a house on the Delacroix *domaine* of St Julien. If the impression she'd gathered over the years was accurate, the estate was a very wealthy one, and her legacy of a house and a modest sum of money was one Armand Delacroix would never miss.

Sadness flickered across Claudie's expressive face. Annelise's death hadn't come as that much of a surprise. She'd been ill for some time and hadn't made her usual visit to Claudie's parents' home for more than two years. Which was why the legacy had come as even more of a surprise. Claudie had had not the smallest hint.

The sadness was washed away by a feeling of warmth and gratitude. The bond between herself and Annelise had always been a strong one. It was her French godmother who had chosen Claudie's name and taken a close interest in her life ever since.

And it wasn't only Claudie who had benefited from Annelise's warm heart and generosity. She had taken Armand Delacroix, the orphaned son of her husband's brother, into her home and her heart at the age of six and reared him as her own. On her death, he had inherited everything, except for Claudie's small legacy. That ought to give them something in common, at least.

'Are you Claudie Drew?'

The question startled her out of her reverie and she blinked up at the dark-haired man, who seemed to tower above her.

She felt the flooding of relief and gave him a smile. 'Yes. Have you come to pick me up?'

'You might say that.'

There was no answering smile in the near-black eyes as they gazed down at her with an intense scrutiny that soon made her feel uncomfortable.

Here really was a stereotype. Tall, dark and undeniably handsome, with a tilt to the attractive head that betrayed arrogance and an awareness of his own cool charm.

Feeling hot, untidy and somewhat at a disadvantage, Claudie stood up and, giving her annoyance a little rein, said coolly, 'Are you the chauffeur?'

'Unfortunately not.' His tone was mildly derisive. 'I'm afraid it's the chauffeur's day off.'

His voice was deep and attractive despite the coolness. His English was almost perfect, but the merest trace of an accent added allure, Claudie noted with a strange little tingle.

'You will have to make do with me. I'm Armand Delacroix.'

Claudie smothered a gasp of dismay. Of course he was. With his looks and bearing he couldn't be anyone else. She was annoyed with herself for not having realised.

Hot colour flooded her cheeks. 'I wasn't expecting you to meet me in person.'

The hint of a smile briefly curved the well-shaped mouth. 'As heiress to some of the Delacroix estate, however modest a part, you are entitled to the courtesy.' He took her hand in his long, lean fingers and kissed it.

His clasp was strong, the touch of his lips against her fingers firm, almost possessive, and for a brief, idiotic moment Claudie felt trapped ... overpowered by some strange magnetism that drew her, despite her fear.

'May I welcome you to St Julien.' His tone was courteous, but lacking in warmth.

'Thank you. Er ... *merci*.' Claudie stuttered a reply, looking up at him in a fluster of uncertainty. The words of welcome weren't echoed in his expression. The near-black eyes were narrowed on her face and distinctly unfriendly.

Claudie's heart sank. She hadn't expected him to be pleased at the prospect of a virtually unknown English girl having a share of his inheritance, but she had hoped he would have reached some degree of reasonable acceptance. From his attitude, it was plain that he hadn't.

He picked up her luggage and said abruptly, 'Shall we go?'

Claudie followed him to the large, sleek saloon car parked near the exit with a sudden little tremor of anticipation. This was the last lap of her journey, and soon she would be face to face with her legacy. A house of her own. Whatever he felt, Armand Delacroix couldn't take that excitement away from her.

Following behind, she could watch him, her eyes ranging, with almost furtive interest, over his tall figure. His broad, muscular frame moved with lithe grace and even in tailored trousers and a casual short-sleeved shirt he had an air of authority that was faintly intimidating.

She had known about him all her life ... thought and speculated about him for all her adolescent years. Which made it all the more startling ... almost unnerving ... to find herself confronted by a complete stranger. And an antagonistic stranger at that!

He stowed her luggage in the boot and then opened the passenger door, indicating that she should get in. Claudie's gaze followed him as he walked around the bonnet to settle himself in at the wheel. Inside the car, he seemed even bigger, his shoulders filling up the space and touching against hers as he strapped himself in and started the engine.

Claudie clipped her belt in place and watched the strong brown hands on the wheel as he manoeuvred the car out of the car park. He had nice hands and for a moment she had a startling vision of them moving against her in slow passion...a vision that had her heart pounding and her brain reeling with incredulity as she wondered where it had come from. Because, in reality, no man's hand had aroused that kind of excitement.

She leaned back and took a deep, steadying breath, turning her attention forcibly to what was going on outside of her head. The bright, attractive little town was practically deserted and all the buildings, the shops and cafés, seemed closed.

'Where is everybody?' Claudie asked, her voice breaking the silence that had built up around them. 'Everything seems so quiet.'

'It's twelve-thirty,' he said. 'The lunch-hour here is from midday until two o'clock and most people go home if they can.'

His tone indicated the end of the conversation and Claudie settled back with a little sigh. Small talk, along with her company, obviously wasn't welcome and she was too tired to push the issue.

The soft leather interior of the air-conditioned car was comfortable and cool after the heat of the day and soon her eyes began to grow heavy and close. As she felt herself drifting off into sleep, she struggled awake, casting him a self-conscious glance, unsure of what

French manners might dictate, but he seemed absorbed in his own thoughts.

She turned her head to look out of the window, watching the countryside rolling by. Away from the town, the road curved and twisted alongside a broad river, gleaming pale gold in the sun. A number of boats were moving in leisurely fashion upstream, between banks that were bordered by surprisingly green, lush fields of un-familiar-looking vegetation.

She wished she could tell him how lovely she found it all, how peaceful, but his air of detachment—or was it boredom?—precluded such friendly confidences.

And in the end she fell asleep, waking in a daze to find herself confronted by a large, rambling dwelling built in the same peach-coloured stone as the station. It almost took her breath away.

'Is this it? My house?'

For a moment, she thought he almost smiled. 'Yes. This is your inheritance.'

Claudie's eyes widened with delight. 'Oh! It's beautiful.'

'Yes.' He opened the car door for her to clamber out and she stood staring at the house in awe, hardly aware that his gaze was fixed firmly on her.

'Annelise called it her mini-château. She loved it very much.'

'I'm sure I will too.' Claudie's tone was reverent. 'Oh! I just can't believe it.'

He said, with what Claudie thought was a touch of irony, 'I'm sure you can't.' Then, as she turned ques-tioning violet eyes on him, he nudged her forward. 'Go in. The door's open. I'll bring your luggage.'

Face to face at last with her inheritance, the reality was far from the snug little cottage of her imagination.

The house was large, quite obviously old, with the original stone remarkably intact, and the whole beautifully maintained. The red roof sloped gently over creamy stonework. Against the brilliant blue sky it gave the effect of a storybook illustration.

Claudie went up the steps, on to the balcony, with a feeling of almost total unreality. She opened the front door and stepped into the hallway with its huge open fireplace and polished wood floors, to become enveloped in a feeling of immediate rapport.

Dimly, she heard the thump of her luggage being dropped and the front door closing.

Wandering into the bright, airy living-room, with its tall windows, beautiful antique furniture and rich rugs, she gave a huge sigh of pure bliss and closed her eyes.

'Oh, Annelise!' she cried softly. 'I never expected anything as lovely as this. I think I must be dreaming. I need someone to pinch me.'

A movement close by startled her into opening her eyes.

Armand Delacroix was there. Lost in her rapture, she'd forgotten about him. He was looking down at her, his near-black eyes strangely intent.

'An odd request,' he said politely. 'Is it some kind of English ritual on entering a new home?'

Claudie gave an embarrassed little laugh. 'Of course not. It's just a figure of speech. I don't really want anyone to pinch me. Not even to convince me of the reality of all this.'

'I'm relieved to hear it. No one should abuse such soft, delicate skin.'

He spoke in a low, strangely vibrant voice, running a finger along her arm, bare in her sleeveless T-shirt, blazing a fiery path against her sensitised skin.

She gave a little shudder and made to turn away, but he caught her arms, drawing her towards him.

'I can think of a much pleasanter way to convince you of reality.'

He dipped his head suddenly and captured her lips with his in a kiss that had Claudie quivering from head to foot. It was slow and thorough and she was breathless when he lifted his mouth from hers. As he moved back, she stared up at him, her lips still parted, burning from the impression of his.

'Well! Did that help?' he queried solemnly.

There was a peculiar light in his dark eyes that did strange things to her insides and made her want to go on staring into them forever. But, with an effort, she tore her gaze away.

After his earlier coldness, it was impossible to understand this change.

Feeling a little dazed, she said, 'I thought you'd left my cases and gone.'

He raised dark brows in astonishment. 'You thought I would go without making sure you have everything you need?'

Beneath her dazed feelings ran a strong undercurrent of anger. 'There's no need for you to worry about that. I'm sure I can find my own way to the local shops.'

He grunted. 'You will find no such luxuries here in the heart of the French countryside, *mademoiselle*. The best you can hope for is a twice-weekly visit from the mobile shop.'

Claudie made an ironic sound. 'Oh, great! Then I may have a long wait.'

'Perhaps not. If Madame Sicre has obeyed her instructions.' He took her hand, suffusing her with a strange warmth, and began guiding her through the living-room and out into a large oak-beamed kitchen lined with carved wooden cupboards.

'I'm sure you'll find everything you need here. If not, then you must say.'

Claudie, releasing her oddly tingling fingers ostentatiously from his grasp, opened the cupboards and stared at the well-stocked shelves. The contents of these cupboards would keep her for a month or more. She felt a surge of antagonism. This apparent evidence of care could only be condescension.

'Thank you,' she muttered tightly. 'I'm sure you mean to be kind, but I don't expect you to keep me, *monsieur*. I can provide for myself.'

'But of course.' His smile disappeared. 'However. Please regard this as a welcoming present.'

Claudie clamped her lower lip in her teeth in case she was tempted to remark that she hadn't noticed any real air of welcome. The kiss he'd just given her had, she was sure, been in the nature of a power game. Not that she could guess what it was meant to achieve. She felt like telling him what he could do with his free gifts.

Instead, she muttered a reluctant, 'Thank you.'

'*C'est mon plaisir.*' He bowed briefly, his dark eyes giving nothing away. 'And, when you run out of provisions, just let me have your list and I'll arrange someone from the main house to pick it up for you.'

The arrogance of the man, she fumed. Why was he treating her this way? With the same kind of exaggerated courtesy one usually extended to an unwelcome visitor. Letting them know you hoped they wouldn't be staying.

Claudie's violet eyes flashed fire. 'Thanks. But that won't be necessary. Since I'm going to be here for some time, I intend to be as self-sufficient as possible. Perhaps I can buy a bicycle or something.'

His unexpected laugh surprised her, full of wry amusement. 'Are you really fit enough to cycle thirty-six kilometers round trip to the nearest supermarket?'

She bit her lip. 'Not at the moment, perhaps. But I'll work on it.'

'No doubt,' he said drily. 'But, until then, remember. I shall be happy to be at your disposal.'

'Thanks again.'

Ignoring her faint sarcasm, he gave her a brief nod.

He turned away and Claudie breathed a sigh of relief, thinking he was about to leave. She was longing to explore the house, to search out the intriguing nooks and crannies she was sure she would find, savouring her good fortune to the full. She could do none of that until he was gone, which hopefully would be soon.

But he walked instead to a window and stared out across the pasture land beyond the small garden.

'Do you think you would be happy here, *mademoiselle*? Tucked away in the countryside?'

Claudie came and stood beside him, looking at the view, with a little inner glow of pride and happiness. This was her new world and no one, not even the powerful Armand Delacroix, was going to spoil things for her.

'I shall be blissfully happy here, *monsieur*. I'm sorry if that disappoints you.'

He turned to her with a heavy frown between his strong arched brows. 'Why should that disappoint me?'

Now he was looking straight at her, Claudie felt her nerve begin to slip a little, but she said bravely, 'Well, despite everything, I can't help feeling you're not happy about the fact that Annelise left this house to me, a complete stranger.'

He made a wry sound. 'Not quite a *complete* stranger, no. I was aware of your existence, of course, but only just.'

She laughed drily. 'Then this legacy was as much of a surprise to you as it was to me.'

'A surprise, yes!' His eyes were cold again and guarded. 'And you? Do you really mean to say that you had no idea?'

She said indignantly, 'Why do you find that so hard to believe? I haven't seen Annelise for three years and, for the last two, she'd written only two or three letters to my mother.'

'And in none of them did she mention the house?' The pupils of his eyes were lost in the glittering dark brown irises and the grooves of his strong face seemed set in iron.

Hiding a shiver, Claudie straightened and stared back at him. 'That's right. Perhaps she wanted to give me a wonderful surprise.'

His dark brows arched sardonically. 'Somewhat out of character, I'd say. Annelise was never that impulsive. Everything she did was for a purpose.'

That was true, Claudie knew. Her godmother had always planned meticulously.

'What I can't be sure of,' he said musingly, 'is her intention in bringing you here to her house.'

She said tightly, 'Can't you just accept it was her final gift to me?'

He laughed cynically. 'A pretty substantial gift, don't you think?'

Frayed by fatigue and hunger and the hostility of this unexpected cross-questioning, her temper finally snapped.

'Yes, I do, as a matter of fact! But I disagree that it was out of character. Annelise was the kindest, most

generous person I've ever known. And if she wanted me
to have this house, then I'm grateful and I intend to live
in it happily whatever you may think of the idea.'

He grasped her shoulders in a fierce grip, his hard
eyes boring into the soft violet of hers, like laser beams
burning into every corner, leaving no shadows.

'It's not what I think, but what I know of Annelise.'
His mouth was a tight, furious line. 'If I thought for
one moment that this had been planned between you,
I'd...'

The steel of his fingers bit more deeply into the soft
flesh of her upper arms, forcing her to cry out, but he
didn't slacken his hold.

'Planned what?' she demanded through clenched
teeth. 'For me to have this house? How many times do
I have to say it's not true? But even if it was, you're not
losing much, are you? With the rest of the estate, you're
more than well provided for. Or do you feel you should
have it all?'

'More to the point,' he said, sounding malevolent, 'do
you?'

Claudie stared at him in confusion. 'I haven't the
slightest idea of what you're talking about.' Then, as the
pain of his grip became unbearable, she tugged fiercely,
trying to pull away. 'If you don't let go of me, I'll...'

The force with which he shook her suddenly from him
had her staggering backwards, stumbling over the thick
rug. His hands shot out to steady her, but she slapped
them away.

'Don't touch me!'

Her teeth were chattering with nerves and she was close
to tears, but she wasn't going to let this beast of a
Frenchman see her weakness.

'If you wouldn't mind leaving now.' Her firm, rounded bosom rose and fell with the force of her anger. 'I'm rather tired.'

Two patches of colour blazed in his tanned cheeks and he seemed to be trying to get his temper under control.

'You must forgive me,' he said at last, in tight, clipped tones. 'I was forgetting my duties as your host.'

She eyed him unrelentingly. 'You are *not* my host. You are my neighbour.' She gave him a tight smile. 'Even so, with any luck, we won't be seeing too much of each other.'

That strange hard glint was back in his eyes. 'You think not?'

Claudie drew a sharp inward breath. 'Let me put it this way. Not if I have anything to do with it.'

He raised dark, arched brows. 'And yet I was just about to say how much I am looking forward to the pleasure of your company at dinner tonight, in the main house. It will be served at nine o'clock.'

She said haughtily, 'Thanks for the invitation, but I'm much too tired after travelling so far.'

He brushed that aside with an imperious hand and said shortly, 'Then you must rest this afternoon. You wouldn't wish to disappoint the family and friends who are so anxious to meet you. Monsieur Previn is travelling down especially for that honour.'

Monsieur Previn was the *notaire* who had contacted Claudie's mother about the legacy. He had been very kind and it was true that she wouldn't want to upset him unnecessarily. Still. This was a matter of pride.

'Another time, perhaps.' She held out her hand. 'Now, if you don't mind, I'll say goodbye.'

He moved back from her, his gaze insolently taking in the flushed cheeks and wide violet eyes, dewy in spite of her anger, the rapid rise and fall of her breasts as she struggled for control.

'Very well. I shall leave you to rest. *Au revoir, mademoiselle.*' He took her hand and kissed it gently, but with a mocking light gleaming in his dark eyes. 'But, I insist you come to dinner. I shall pick you up at eight-thirty.' Giving her no chance to argue further, he lifted his lean hand in a little salute. '*A bientôt!*'

CHAPTER TWO

AFTER he'd left, Claudie sank down into a lovely old armchair and closed her eyes, waiting for the tumult of her feelings to subside.

What was it about that man that made her so angry and yet so weak? Why hadn't she put up more of a fight and told him she would be damned if she'd meekly attend his dinner?

In her mind's eye, she met again that hard, intimidating stare and recoiled. His was the power of the unknown and there was no telling whether she would ever win a battle against him.

In her dreams he had been gentle and thoughtful... moulded by her imagination into her ideal lover. But now, the Armand Delacroix of her innocent adolescent fantasies had vanished forever, to be replaced by an enigma that even her fertile imagination could never have created.

But she had no intention of simply lying down and letting him trample all over her. She would have to give in gracefully this once and go to his dinner tonight, since other people would be involved whom it was possible a refusal might offend. But, once it was over, she had every intention of fighting against his manipulations.

But, lying in the bath later, she found she was still thinking about him. He couldn't know how she'd been looking forward to seeing him. To putting a face at last to the shadowy figure she'd known for so long, but only by name.

He'd been a grown man when she'd been a child, and so he would hardly be likely to take note of Annelise's fond talk of her little god-daughter. How surprised he would be to learn that she herself had paid avid attention when Annelise had been talking about him...her beloved Armand. To her godmother's fond, but sometimes exasperated, monologues on that fascinating subject, Claudie had made a captivated audience.

Over the years, she'd built up her own picture of Armand Delacroix, the secrecy of that image only adding to the thrill of her possession of him...her secret lover. She had never dreamt, in the fervour of her romantic innocence, that one day they would come face to face and she would find herself in his arms, with his mouth covering hers in reality. Remembering that brief kiss, she felt her lips burn with the fiery touch...sensual enough to make a young girl giddy, perhaps. But that girl had finally grown up. Which was just as well, she thought wryly.

She gave herself a mental shake and rubbed soap vigorously on to her slim legs.

Claudie had forgotten to alter her watch and it was a shock to realise that she had less than an hour to get ready for dinner.

She'd slept soundly for too long. She hadn't even had time to unpack and sort out her clothes.

Rummaging through her cases now, she tried frantically to remember what she had eventually packed. Evening wear hadn't seemed very high on her priority list at the time.

She threw one garment after another impatiently on the bed, before drawing out a gown she'd made up herself for the last arts ball. A gossamer-light concoction, jewel-bright with all the colours of the rainbow. She eyed it doubtfully. At the time, alongside all the way-out gear favoured by her friends and classmates, it had appeared almost conservative. Now, it seemed positively to shout for attention.

It clung to her curves, making her look taller and elegant in a willowy way. And the mixture of colours, which normally she avoided, came together to complement her smooth pale skin and to bring out the bluer tones of her violet eyes.

Even though she rushed her toilette, she was still putting the final touches to her make-up as the brass bell at her front door sounded, heralding the arrival of Armand Delacroix.

Flustered, she flew down the stairs to open the door to him, her cheeks tinged pink with exertion.

'Come in,' she said, as he stood in the doorway, his dark eyes unreadable in the soft light of dusk. 'I'm not quite ready. I slept too long.'

He stepped inside, dropping a light kiss on each cheek, before laying cool fingers against her hot skin, surprising her with the gentleness of his touch. 'Don't rush, *mademoiselle*. I'm sure the other guests won't mind waiting a little.'

She frowned, searching his face for sarcasm, but as usual his expression was enigmatic.

'Please, go in and sit down.' She indicated the living-room with a hand which was unaccountably shaking. 'I'm just putting the final touches.'

'To an already perfect picture, *mademoiselle*? No final touch is necessary.'

To her annoyance, she felt her cheeks grow hot again under his dark scrutiny and she tore her gaze away, dashing for the staircase.

'Thanks,' she said over her shoulder. 'Shan't keep you a moment.'

Back in her bedroom, she had to fight to recover her
breath. He looked devastating in a dark dinner suit and
the sight of his cool, handsome features was still sending
ricochets of sensations through her body.

With trembling hands, she put long crystal pendants
in her ears which reflected the colours of her dress like
a prism. She sprayed on a little of her favourite perfume.
Her cheeks still bore traces of hectic colour and she
waited for it to recede before finally descending the stairs
again.

'You look enchanting,' he said, and offered her his
hand.

After only a brief hesitation, she took it, stifling a
gasp as the warm current of his vitality flowed strongly
through her, growing in intensity as he lifted her fingers
to his mouth in a brief kiss.

She supposed she would have to get used to this odd
intimacy of strangers which was part of the French way
of life. But she had a strong suspicion that he was making
the most of the opportunities it presented.

As her gaze flickered uncertainly on his, he smiled, a
wide, sensuous curving movement of his lips that increased her discomfort still further. Despite her dislike,
her awareness of him was so intense as to leave her
speechless.

With her hand tucked into the crook of his arm, she
let him lead her to the car.

If Claudie had been astonished by her own house, the
main house overwhelmed her. She supposed it was the
equivalent of a large English mansion, with an avenue
of strangely stunted trees leading up to an impressive
entrance, surrounded by extensive gardens in full and
glorious bloom.

A wide, curving flight of pinkish stone steps led up to the large carved wooden door, at which stood an elderly woman dressed in black, with a bunch of keys at her waist that must have weighed several pounds.

The woman spoke austerely and unintelligibly to Claudie, who could only manage a smile in reply.

As they entered the house, Armand's dark eyes were teasingly on hers. 'You do *speak* French, *mademoiselle*?'

'Yes, of course,' she replied, sounding huffy. 'But it's a bit rusty.'

He said a little grimly, 'Then polish it up. You'll need it.'

Pausing in the doorway of the magnificent drawing-room, where a small group of people stood, obviously awaiting the arrival of their host and the girl from England, Claudie felt a moment's panic.

Never in her life before had her colour fluctuated so often or so easily, she thought, as she felt the tide rising again. The flush that mounted her cheeks must have matched the scarlet in the rainbow gown as she walked, with as much dignity as she could muster, the length of the long room to the fireplace, where the guests had congregated.

Every eye was turned in her direction, she noted in acute embarrassment, as Armand Delacroix took her arm, leading her forward for the introductions.

'We are a little late.' He spoke in French, drawing her into the group with a firm light hand against her waist. The touch was somehow reassuring and Claudie breathed a little easier. 'Mademoiselle Drew was unavoidably de-layed,' he said. 'She hopes for your forgiveness.'

'Yes. I hadn't altered my watch and...' she rushed in nervously and then ground to a halt, silenced by the lift of his authoritative hand.

'No matter,' he said courteously. 'I'm sure everyone was pleased to wait.'

Claudie clenched her hands tightly together. Had he had to make such an issue of it? After all, it was he who had said they wouldn't mind waiting. Resentment flared in her, until she realised, seeing the curiosity lingering still in the eyes turned upon them, that he'd had to offer his waiting guests some explanation for their late arrival. And by cutting her short he had probably saved her from some kind of social gaffe.

Shooting a hesitant glance up at him, she caught the briefest of smiles and for a second his hand tightened against her waist before he released her. Without that small measure of support, she felt strangely forlorn.

'Before we eat, let me first introduce you.' He waved a lean hand. 'Monsieur Previn you must already know.'

The thin man beside Claudie inclined his head in a bow and she was amused to see the *notaire* looked just the way she had imagined he would, with a thin, pinched face and sparse dark hair.

'We have spoken only by telephone,' he said in carefully precise French. 'And I have been looking forward to this meeting.'

He extended a bony hand, which she clasped briefly with a murmured greeting. There was the glimmer of sincerity in the sombre eyes that made Claudie glad she hadn't stubbornly refused to come. Armand had been right to insist after all.

The other guests were the local doctor and his wife, Monsieur and Madame Valette, and a dark-haired girl with classically beautiful features, introduced as Miranda Belling, who acknowledged Claudie's halting French in cool, clipped English, while appraising her from beneath dark fringed lashes.

Claudie returned her regard with suppressed curiosity. English, like herself, and evidently unfriendly. Claudie wondered why.

'Miranda was formerly Annelise's personal secretary,' Armand explained, as though in answer to her silent question. 'But, at her own request, she has stayed on and is now secretary to the estate.'

Intercepting the charged glance the girl shot in his direction, Claudie wondered if that was all she was. It obviously wasn't all she *wanted* to be, she thought in wry amusement.

Armand Delacroix appeared oblivious to whatever message the large grey eyes were sending him, as he waved his hand once more at a dark-haired young man who had been standing a little apart from the group.

'And this ... is my cousin Pascal Dubret.'

He was darker-skinned than Armand, with thick, tightly curling hair and heavily hooded brown eyes. He moved forward to kiss her cheeks. 'We have all been waiting, with great impatience, for your arrival in France, *mademoiselle*,' he said, in thickly accented English.

'How nice.' Claudie turned her smile on him.

She saw the frown which passed like a shadow over Armand Delacroix's handsome face, before a cool smile took its place.

By contrast, Pascal's thin face was positively beaming. 'My cousin, in particular, has been most anxious to see you. Now that he has pacified some of his fears, and has you under his wing at last, I'm sure he can feel happy.'

Claudie murmured uncomfortably, 'Thank you. But I don't wish anyone to feel responsible for me.'

'But of course we are responsible,' Pascal insisted. 'As Annelise's god-daughter you are one of the family, *mademoiselle*. A partner in the estate, which you must

think of as completely at your disposal.' He turned dark,
amused eyes on his cousin. 'Isn't that so, Armand?'

Claudie, picking up the obvious note of sarcasm in
Pascal's voice, shot a hesitant little glance at her host,
remembering the rather fraught incident earlier in the
day. Was this what it had all been about? Did he fear
her unwarranted intrusion into his family life?

Well, he would soon see that he need have nothing to
fear on that score.

'Hardly a partner, Monsieur Dubret,' she said tightly,
aware that the eyes of the other guests were turned closely
upon them. 'I'm more than happy just to have my house
and to leave you in peace. You need hardly know I'm
here.'

'Ah! But that would be terrible!' Pascal disclaimed
with a wave of his thin hand. 'I, for one, am very pleased
to have you here at St Julien and I should feel honoured
to show you around the *domaine*. We have a delightful
swimming-pool. You will probably want to swim there
every day in this climate.'

'I love to swim, of course.' Claudie was beginning to
feel desperately uncomfortable. 'But I hardly think
Monsieur Delacroix would be happy for me to make such
use of his facilities.'

Pascal's lips twisted in a crooked smile. 'The facilities
are not yet Armand's to command, but I know he will
be most eager to accommodate you. Isn't that so,
cousin?'

The people grouped around them were suddenly still
and it would have been possible to have heard a pin drop
into the oddly fraught silence.

The eyes of the two men met in an obvious contest of
wills that seemed to have everyone holding their breath.

Armand spoke at last. 'Mademoiselle Drew is, of
course, welcome to swim in the pool if she wishes.'

Claudie glanced from one to the other, disconcerted by the tension that was practically tangible in the air between them.

Pascal said, in a soft voice, 'And welcome to much more, if it gains the advantage you seek. Eh, Armand?'

Armand's taut face became suffused with colour against which the dark eyes glittered dangerously. 'This is hardly the time or place to display the strange quirks of your reasoning, Pascal. The meal has been delayed enough. I suggest we take our places at the dinner table and commence.'

Pascal smiled tightly. 'By all means. Let us commence.'

A sigh of relief seemed to pass around the assembly as they were led into the imposing dining-room.

To her further discomfort, Claudie found she was seated beside Armand Delacroix at the head of the table, with Monsieur Previn to her right. Miranda Belling sat opposite between the doctor and Pascal, with the doctor's wife the other side of the *notaire*. They all seemed tense and notably ill at ease.

What on earth was going on? Claudie wondered. Armand Delacroix obviously resented her arrival, as did Miranda Belling. And Pascal, although appearing to welcome her, seemed intent on using her as some kind of weapon against his cousin.

Not a very auspicious beginning to her sojourn in France, she commented silently, stifling a sigh, as she began on the soup.

Despite her earlier hunger, Claudie found herself quite unable to match the appetites of her dinner companions. As course followed course, the evening seemed to stretch endlessly ahead.

Claudie's French proved to be more rusty than she'd thought and it was a struggle to keep up a conversation with the ponderous *notaire*.

Still, it helped to distract her from the powerful awareness of her handsome host. Much to her relief, he spoke to her only occasionally, being engrossed in a discussion with the doctor. But from time to time she was painfully conscious of his muscled thigh, brushing lightly against hers beneath the table, as he moved in his seat.

She tried to avoid the touch of his hand as he passed dishes. The live current which flowed between them when his fingers accidentally made contact with hers had her gasping with astonishment. But if he felt the charge, he gave no indication of it. Trying to hide her own responses, Claudie paid even closer attention to Monsieur Previn's discourse on the beauties of the region.

'Is it, perhaps, too early to ask what you think of the countryside, *mademoiselle*?'

'I'm enchanted. It seemed to me that the further south you come, the more beautiful the landscape. I hope to explore more closely once I've settled in.'

Monsieur Previn nodded gravely. 'So! You intend to spend some time here, *non*?'

She nodded. 'I intend to live here, at least for as long as the money lasts out.'

His thin-lipped smile seemed one of approval. '*Bon*! Then happily we shall have the pleasure of your company for some little time to come.'

Well, I've made one friend at least, she thought ironically.

Catching the chilly eye of Miranda Belling, she found herself wishing she could have met with the same acceptance from other quarters.

Monsieur Previn's rather formal French was easier to understand than the fast-flowing conversations going on around her, but, even so, her responses called for a great deal of concentration, which she soon found fatiguing.

She barely managed to smother her yawns and was surprised, on turning her head discreetly aside yet again, to find she was looking into Armand Delacroix's dark eyes, which were unexpectedly full of amusement.

'I did warn you, *mademoiselle*, that you would need to brush up on your French. It seems a lot of brushing will be necessary.'

He spoke softly in English, leaning so that his mouth was close to her ear, his breath tantalising soft tendrils of hair against her cheek. 'Very few of our local people speak English, and the regional accent is even more difficult.'

Claudie grimaced. 'Thanks. That's cheered me up.'

He laughed, a pleasant sound that tingled through her senses.

'I'm glad to see that something can.'

Claudie opened her mouth to comment that he hadn't made much effort in that direction so far, but he moved away as a maid came between them to serve the next course.

Claudie eyed it with dismay. She felt full to bursting point already. But at last the meal was finished and they all moved to the adjacent sitting-room for coffee.

Her legs had begun to feel a little wobbly and she found herself a seat on a sofa placed against the wall, wishing she knew how much longer she would be expected to stay. Since Armand Delacroix was the host and she presumed he would also be the one to drive her back to her house, she could hardly hurry matters by requesting to be excused. She supposed she would just have to wait until he was ready to take her.

Her spirits sank still lower when Miranda Belling sat down beside her, a smile on her lovely face that didn't quite reach her cool grey eyes.

'So you're planning on staying, Miss Drew.'

The secretary had obviously been listening in to Claudie's conversation with Monsieur Previn.

'Yes. That's the general idea.' Claudie tried to keep the dislike out of her voice. There was something about this girl that put her teeth on edge.

Miranda settled herself more comfortably, crossing one long leg over the other, smoothing her elegant dress to display the contours of a shapely thigh.

'It's very quiet here in the French countryside. Coming from London, you might find it too quiet.'

'I don't think so. I was brought up in the country. My parents moved to London when I was twelve. I've often wished they hadn't.'

Miranda nodded politely. 'All the same, if you do decide to go back home, you can always rent out your house to summer holidaymakers. Lots of English people do.'

Claudie felt a stab of annoyance. The girl was quite blatant in her attempt to get rid of a prospective rival.

'You aren't tempted to go home yourself, then? I'm sure you're a girl who likes the bright lights.'

Miranda's smile grew silky. 'Yes. But I find them in Paris. Armand and I travel up regularly.'

Claudie's stretched nerves were chafed by the girl's smug air of possession.

'I see. One of the perks of the job, no doubt.'

Why do I feel so bitchy? Claudie asked herself vexedly. I'm sure I don't care what Armand Delacroix gets up to in his spare time.

Miranda said smoothly, 'That's right. Among others.'

Claudie responded drily, 'Lucky you. But, for myself, I think I'll just stay at home, brush up on my French, and become one of the locals.'

Miranda's gasp was clearly audible and her face turned pale beneath her light tan.

'Try it!' she said in a voice that was almost a hiss. 'But you won't win. I was here first and Armand is clever enough to have seen through your little scheme. Annelise didn't know him as well as she thought she did.'

'I wouldn't know,' Claudie replied, unable to hide her astonishment. 'But, even if true, I don't see what it would have to do with me. Or with you either for that matter.'

'Don't you?' The girl's laugh was low and venomous. 'I'm not easily fooled, Miss Drew. In fact, if you choose to carry on with the game, you'll find me always one jump ahead.'

Claudie stared at her, her mouth slightly open, wishing she indeed knew what kind of game these people were playing.

'Are you planning a race, perhaps, Miss Belling?' Armand Delacroix's voice cut in, with a steely edge that reflected in the cold dark depths of his eyes. 'Or competition of another kind?'

Miranda's face flushed dull red, adding an unexpected coarseness to her perfect features.

'No, of course not.' She was obviously put out by his unexpected intrusion. 'I was just explaining . . .'

She was halted by the lift of an imperious hand. 'Thank you. But any explaining there is to be done will be done by me.' His eyes narrowed on her hot face. 'I think you know my views on gossip. From my confidential secretary I demand absolute discretion.'

'Yes, but I wasn't . . . I mean . . . I haven't . . .' She faltered, her grey eyes bright with a suspicion of tears as they were caught in his unbending gaze. Turning on her heel, she left them.

Claudie was surprised by a feeling of sympathy for the girl.

'She wasn't gossiping,' she said coolly, as Armand sat down beside her. 'Merely engaging in a little unnecessary sparring.' She found herself adding drily, 'I think Miss Belling's fallen victim to your charms.'

This close, his presence was overwhelming. He eyed her calmly and, caught in the depth of his dark gaze, Claudie felt her heartbeat alter rhythm.

Sounding amused, he said, 'But you quite obviously haven't, Mademoiselle Drew.'

Claudie's expression was cynical. 'How observant of you, Monsieur Delacroix.'

He smiled a slow smile that had her heart unexpectedly fluttering and leaned confidentially towards her. 'There is yet still time, *ma chérie*.' His hand covered hers where it lay in her lap. 'And we shall see.'

His dark eyes held an expression of such determined intensity that it had Claudie sucking in her breath and wondering dizzily why she felt so weak.

What had he meant—we shall see?

In a matter of minutes, she had endured two conversations that had completely mystified her, each with an undercurrent it was impossible to define. Of the two, Armand had shaken her the most. It was one thing to cross swords with Miranda Belling for the fun of it, but clashing openly with the charismatic Frenchman was quite a different kettle of fish.

His attention was still fixed firmly on her in slow appraisal. 'I haven't yet had an opportunity to compliment you on your appearance, *mademoiselle*. Such a beautiful gown.'

'I'm glad you like it.'

'I more than like it. I'm enchanted. The style... it is so unusual.' His voice was warm... faintly teasing. 'In it, you look as exotically lovely as a butterfly.'

Claudie looked up, flushing faintly at the gleam of obvious admiration in his near-black eyes.

She said a little shyly, 'It's one of my own designs.'

His lean hand fingered the delicate material and Claudie felt a tremor as though his touch were against her bare skin.

'Then you have a rare talent. If you have more designs, I should like to see them.'

Claudie frowned. Was this some kind of chat-up line? The reverse, perhaps, of, Come up and see my etchings?

The doctor was signalling his departure, and Claudie let go of her breath in a sigh of relief as Armand, with a faintly irritable sound, rose, excused himself, and moved across the room.

She stood up restlessly, brushing out the creases in her dress. The party, it seemed, was about to break up and soon she would be able to take her departure. The evening hadn't exactly been an easy one.

Pascal appeared suddenly at her elbow, bringing with him a subtle air of disturbance. He'd obviously been eavesdropping.

'I agree with my cousin, *mademoiselle*. The gown is delightful. And you are indeed as lovely as a butterfly.'

He came closer, his voice dropping almost to a whisper. 'But beware! You must take care not to be caught in a net. Particularly not that of my cousin.'

He flicked a malicious glance in the direction of Armand, who seemed to sense his regard, returning it with cold disdain.

Claudie sighed. 'Why do you two fight so much? And why do you keep trying to draw me into it?'

'When you know that, *ma belle*, you will have the answer to the riddle.'

'I hate riddles,' Claudie fretted. 'Please answer me.'

'Not yet.' He shook his head, his eyes gleaming with malice. 'For the moment, I am content to watch the sport.'

A trickle of ice ran down her spine. 'What sport?'

Claudie saw, with a start of dismay, that Armand was crossing the room towards them.

'Saying your goodbyes, Pascal?' he questioned politely, though the dark eyes bored like lasers into those of his cousin. 'I understand you leave us for Paris in the morning.'

'Unfortunately, yes. I am sure you will be glad of the respite, but I regret it now that Mademoiselle Drew has arrived.' Pascal's thin smile broadened. 'I have just been adding my compliments to yours. She is indeed very beautiful.'

Both men eyed Claudie, making her flush with indignation.

But they were too concerned with their battle to notice her stormy expression.

'I'm sure Mademoiselle Drew is quite capable of discerning the genuine from the merely suave, cousin.'

Pascal gave a short, unamused laugh. 'I certainly hope so. If only for her sake.'

Armand's brows lowered darkly. 'Quite so. Now if you'll excuse me.'

Claudie felt the tight grip of his hand against her elbow and turned to look up at him. His face was taut with restrained anger.

'Come,' he said tersely. 'I'm sure you're tired. I will see you home.'

She breathed a sigh of relief.

The short drive back to her house was accomplished almost in silence. She could feel the tension in Armand's body as it brushed against hers in the confines of the car. He was obviously still furious at Pascal.

She sat quietly, trying to make sense of what had gone on during the evening. In retrospect, everyone had appeared to be searching for some kind of response from her. The *notaire* had seemed pleased she was staying. Miranda obviously wanted her to go and Armand and Pascal had treated her like a bone between two dogs. Why?

Arriving at Claudie's house, Armand got out of the car to escort her to the front door, but, to her relief, didn't seem to expect to be asked in.

'I won't keep you further from your rest.'

He leaned forward to kiss her cheeks and Claudie breathed in his subtle male scent with secret excitement, followed by self-disgust. She wasn't a daydreaming schoolgirl any more. In reality, his magnetism was far more potent than her immature heart could have imagined and that subtle scent inexplicably signalled danger.

She said, more coolly than she'd intended, '*Bonne nuit*, Monsieur Delacroix. And thank you for an ... interesting evening.'

His dark eyes held a spark of amusement. 'Interesting! I'm sure! But I hope we shall spend many far more pleasurable evenings together.'

Claudie's heart skipped a beat at his implication, but her tone was stiff. After all, he had accused her of wanting more than was her due. 'Don't let me impose on your time, *monsieur*. It isn't my intention to intrude into your life.'

He said, with a return of that cynicism she disliked so much, 'You are in my life, *mademoiselle*. Courtesy of Annelise. I'm not in danger of forgetting that fact.'

'If it still annoys you so much, then forget about me,' she said with a flare of temper, born of dead hope. Despite everything, the strange resentment was still in him.

He shook his head. 'Even to try would be impossible.'

He was close, looking down at her with those inscrutable dark eyes that both fascinated and infuriated her.

'*Non, chérie*! We shall meet again soon. I promise.'

Claudie wanted to shout, No! No! No! To tell him that already she felt he was a danger to her equilibrium. But, at some illogical level, she was aware of a stir of excitement at the thought of seeing him again.

Pascal had been right to warn her.

Having been close enough, all evening, to feel the pull of Armand's magnetic personality, she'd begun to suspect it was a net into which it might be easy to fall. And if she was to find the peace of mind she was seeking here in France, she must not allow that to happen.

Pride alone should keep her from joining the ranks of the women who had loved and lost Armand Delacroix.

CHAPTER THREE

CLAUDIE spent the early part of the morning unpacking her clothes. They looked a pathetically meagre collection hanging in the vast wardrobes that had once housed Annelise's beautiful apparel.

She wondered what had happened to the gorgeous collection. The chic creations had always seemed an integral part of her godmother's elegant, warm personality. Somehow, it was sad to think they had vanished too.

She gave herself a mental shake. The last thing Annelise would want would be for anyone to brood on the past. She always looked to the future, while living each day of the present to the full.

Determinedly, she turned her concentration on to the task in hand.

She was in the cellar, sorting out the crates of her belongings she'd had sent on ahead, when the large old brass bell sounded to announce a visitor.

He was standing in the hallway as she came rushing up to confront him, and it wasn't only the dash up the steep steps that had her breathless.

His looks were as stunning as the first time she'd seen him. He looked startlingly attractive. Immaculate, as always, in an ice-blue and navy striped shirt with close-fitting blue jeans. His handsome face was more relaxed this morning, she noted a little irritably, while she felt as though she'd just run the hundred-yards sprint.

'*Ça va?*' He bent his tall frame to kiss her.

'*Ça va bien*! *Merci*!'

Her cheeks were hot and dusty and she knew there were cobwebs in her hair. She raked her fingers self-consciously through it, thinking she must look like one of the hired hands.

Her voice sounded high and sharp. 'I see you let yourself in.'

He appraised her with calm amusement. 'The front door was open and there was no reply to the bell. I didn't think you'd mind if I came in.'

Claudie frowned up at him. Damn the man! He knew quite well that she minded. It was proving difficult, if not impossible, to keep him at a comfortable distance.

'I suppose you were quite used to coming and going here when Annelise was alive,' she said forthrightly. 'But actually, I did hear the bell and came as quickly as I could.'

He nodded gravely. 'Then next time I shall wait a little more patiently.'

Necessary point made! But, somehow she had little satisfaction from this courteous surrender.

With a sigh, she stood back. 'Won't you come through?'

She led the way to the living-room, where, with the same annoyingly proprietorial air, he seated himself on the sofa nearest to the large stone fireplace, his long denim-clad legs stretched out before him and crossed nonchalantly at the ankle.

It was a compelling sight, she silently grudged. Everything about him did strange things to her insides and she had to look away before her excitement became visible.

But her voice was revealingly husky. 'Can I get you some coffee or something?'

'Coffee would be fine.'

Claudie felt flustered by the enigmatic light in his dark eyes. The whole room seemed full of his presence and it was strangely difficult to breathe. She was glad of the excuse to escape to the kitchen.

When she came back with the tray, he was lounging back, his arm resting along the back of the settee.

'You look very comfortable,' she said pointedly.

He nodded. 'This house has always made me feel that way.' He gave her a smile that was unexpectedly friendly. 'Nothing has changed in that respect.'

He reached forward and took the tray from her, placing it on the low table in front of him. A teasing light glowed in his eyes.

'If you would like to sit, I will be mother. Isn't that the expression?'

She sat beside him and fumed as he handed her one of the tiny cups. He was making fun of her Englishness, she knew. But gently, and somehow that added fuel to her irritation.

'Is this a social call? Or do you have something in particular you want to talk about?'

'A little of both.' He nodded. 'But first, we will drink and maybe get to know each other a little better.'

She sipped at her coffee, her eyes meeting his challengingly above the rim of the tiny cup.

'I had a feeling when we met that you knew me as well as you wanted to. I haven't changed. Have you?'

His eyes narrowed. 'If I was discourteous to you then I apologise. There were certain things I wished to know and there was no way to find out without asking bluntly.'

'You were certainly blunt,' she agreed coolly. 'And were you satisfied with the result of your questioning, or have you brought a bright light to shine into my eyes while you pursue your interrogation?'

He laughed. 'Oh, come, Claudie! You exaggerate.'

'Not at all.'

She tossed her head haughtily, refusing to be distracted by the unexpectedly familiar use of her name.

'You seemed to think I was involved in some kind of intrigue with Annelise to do you out of your inheritance.'

'You are wrong, *chérie*.'

She glimpsed the iron behind that attractive appearance, as he added grimly, 'Nothing can do me out of my inheritance.'

'Good!' Claudie applauded. 'And I certainly don't want to. So now, perhaps, we can forget about it.'

He shook his head, his mouth suddenly grim. 'If that were only possible. But soon, maybe...' He shrugged and spread his lean hands in dismissal of the subject. 'But you, *mademoiselle*! You have been busy this morning?'

'Yes.'

Claudie was secretly as glad as he to drop the subject in favour of something more comfortable.

'I've been sorting through my work materials. And actually I think the cellar would make a good workshop. It would need a window and some stronger lights, but I'm sure that won't be difficult. I'll make do with a room up here in the house until it's ready. I'm quite anxious to make a start.'

She was rambling, she realised with annoyance. How was it his silent regard had the power to reduce her to a babbling schoolgirl? she wondered resentfully.

His brows arched over the penetrating dark eyes. 'So soon? Don't you wish to take a little time to explore your new environment?'

'Perhaps in between times,' she said tightly, drawn into continuing with the conversation she'd unthinkingly commenced. 'But at the moment my priority is to start on some fashion designs I've been working around in my head. The ideas get a little stale if you leave them too long.'

He nodded solemnly. 'And what a pity that would be. If the gown you wore last night is any true indication of your talent, then to neglect such fresh and original ideas would be a crime.'

Claudie, still doubtful about the genuineness of his interest, searched his expression for irony, but he seemed perfectly sincere and she found herself responding.

'I don't know how truly typical the rainbow gown is, but I could show you some of my other designs, if you're really interested.'

'I would be enchanted. In fact, such an honour was the other reason for my visit.'

She laughed wryly. 'Look at them first before you decide whether or not it's an honour.'

He helped her carry the portfolios up from the cellar and to spread the thick sheets of paper out on the long dining-room table. He studied them for some considerable time, a little frown between his dark brows, putting a number aside for further inspection.

He was close, his bare arm brushing hers occasionally as he moved the papers about.

At last he said quietly, 'Your work is good. Some of these designs have great immediacy. You are right to want to press ahead.' He smiled a little grimly. 'Ideas have a perverse way of filtering out into the atmosphere and entering other minds almost at the same time. You must put your name to these quickly.'

Claudie felt a rush of pleasure. Her designs had been well received at college, but had yet to be tested out in the tough world of commerce. It was very gratifying to have a favourable assessment from a man of Armand's obvious acumen.

'It's very nice of you to say so.' Her voice sounded husky with embarrassment. 'But I don't know whether anyone with any real knowledge of the fashion world would have the same opinion.'

He gave her a narrow-eyed smile. 'Believe me, *chérie*, I have reason to know they would.'

Claudie's face coloured with secret excitement. Poised on the edge of her future career, she had been diffident, almost afraid to hope her love of fashion designing would yield her a living. But, perhaps, with Armand's encouragement to sustain her...?

She felt a new surge of confidence and said, with a little laugh, 'I hardly know how to begin, but I do have one or two contacts in London who might be interested.'

'And I have any number of important contacts in Paris who I know would be interested.' His tone was decisive. 'You will begin by making up a portfolio of your best designs, and when they are ready——' he touched the tip of her nose with his finger in a teasing gesture '—we shall see.'

Claudie tempered her pleasure with reserve. 'I'm not expecting a meteoric climb to fame. I'm quite happy to work my way up the ladder one rung at a time.'

He laughed. 'How modest you are, *chérie*.' He brushed his cool lips unexpectedly against hers, making her heart pound. 'Your talent, once noticed, will lead you up quickly and entirely by its own merit.'

He took her hand between his cool ones, holding it in one palm and stroking it lightly with the other. The effect was so erotic that Claudie found it hard to concentrate on her argument.

'I was brought up to believe that success brings satisfaction only through personal achievement.'

'I agree.' He nodded sagely. 'But it surely won't detract from your satisfaction to have the interest and advice of someone a little...more experienced.' The pause seemed pregnant with meaning she was at a loss to grasp. 'Someone who is, perhaps, able to help you avoid the pitfalls and point you in the most likely direction towards success.'

'Meaning you?' Claudie queried in astonishment, her scepticism returning. 'One day you hate the idea of me being here and today you are, I think, offering to help launch me on my career. I can't imagine why, unless you're hoping I'll ship myself off to Paris out of your way.'

He laughed. 'Hardly that, since I shall be in Paris myself most of the time.' He took the hand he was holding to his lips.

She snatched it away, unable to bear the frustration of the sensations he was arousing.

'Then why?'

'Perhaps I was hoping to see you there?'

'Were you?'

For a moment, his eyes met hers, deep, dark and mysterious pools of near promise. Claudie felt herself shudder.

He said softly, 'But of course. I should be delighted to see you anywhere.'

His answer was somehow disappointing.

'Except at St Julien.'

He turned away in sudden impatience. 'You must not imagine what is not there, *chérie*.' He turned back abruptly and grasped her arms. 'You are not what I was expecting. *Non*! And your presence here is a complication which, for personal reasons, I still find it hard to accept. Nevertheless ...' he drew her closer '... there is an enchantment in your eyes that I find hard to ignore. It is as if I have looked into them many times before, though that cannot be.' His arms closed about her. 'And if the eyes promise so much, then what rapture, of fate's devising, remains to be experienced . . . ?'

There was magic in his voice, allure in the dark eyes and sensuous lips poised over hers, but Claudie would allow herself to surrender to neither.

'It is not my imagination that tells me you don't want me. You've made it all too plain. And what possible harm can I do to you?' She tried to shake herself free of him, but he held her with hands of steel. With a little grunt of frustration, she went on, 'And what you've just said makes no sense to me at all.'

'Ah, *chérie*!' He brushed his fingers tantalisingly across her lips and smiled. 'As always, you try to make sense. But who looks for sense in the power of attraction, sweet Claudie? And as for harm...!' He sighed deeply. 'I think the harm is already done.'

Without warning, he was kissing her passionately, his hands hard on her back, his mouth devouring, with a kind of hunger, the softness of hers.

Claudie fought him, pulled desperately to be free of the power that was threatening to overwhelm her.

'Let me go!' she cried, as he paused to take a breath.

'Why should I?' he demanded. 'You are part of my inheritance.' He kissed her fiercely and then spoke again in a strangely ragged voice. 'Annelise bequeathed you to me. Like it or not, it is so.'

The fire in his dark eyes threatened to consume her and she closed her own in an act of self-defence. He took the gesture for surrender and groaned, drawing her tight against him, crushing his lips against hers, draining the strength from her already weakened body.

'You are talking in riddles again,' she protested, but strange fires had ignited inside her, searing through the remnants of her resistance. Desperately, she said, 'Please listen to me!'

He sighed and she felt the movement of his breath, a warm current of excitement, through her own body.

'I am listening, *chérie*. To your heart…which doesn't lie.'

His lips claimed hers once more and she was lost, her rounded breasts crushed against his chest, where their heartbeats seemed to merge in a crescendo of excitement. His hands slid up her back, tracing the supple line of her spine, and down to the slender curve of her waist, the gentle swell of her buttocks. A deep shudder ran through her as he tightened his hold, the hardness of him pressing against the softness of her stomach, making her aware of the strength of his desire.

He lifted his mouth from hers, to move tantalisingly against her sensitive ears, along the line of her arched throat. Brushing the straps of her dress from her shoulders, he moved down towards her breasts, which were taut with heated anticipation. The loose dress slipped lower, baring the swollen evidence of her own desire.

She groaned as his lips touched the sensitive peaks and gripped his head to prevent the sweet torture and pull his face back up to hers.

'Armand. Stop! Please stop!' she groaned.

He made a sound of frustration, his eyes meeting hers with dark, smoky intensity.

'I want you! And I need never stop making love to you.' The words seemed like a vow as he paused before going on, his voice strong and ragged. 'Never, Claudie, *mon amour*, if you would marry me!'

Claudie felt numb with shock. She tried to drag her gaze from his, but he held her still.

'Will you?'

She shook her head fiercely. 'This is ridiculous. You hardly know me.'

'I know enough to begin. The real knowing comes later in a lasting relationship.'

She stared at him, her large violet eyes wide with disbelief.

'That's the kind of relationship you want?'

A memory flashed into her mind of Annelise speaking despairingly of her doubts that her darling Armand would ever find a woman he would want to marry.

'I can't believe you really do want to be married?'

He said drily, putting her a little away from him so that he could see her face, which she knew she was flushed with confusion, 'It appears the time has finally come for that.'

'But, why me?' she persisted, her mind in turmoil.

His eyes locked into hers, intense and unreadable. 'It's what I have been asking myself, *chérie*. But perhaps the time for questions is past. Now I need only your answer.' He came close, speaking almost in a whisper. 'Say you will marry me?'

His dark eyes burned bright with temptation and she closed her own to shut out the light.

Her head buzzed, as though inhabited by a million bees, making her thoughts hard to decipher above the sound.

'No!' she cried, at last. And then, despairingly, 'Oh, God! I don't know!'

'You are not sure?' He made a soft sound of frustration.

'I need time to think.' Her voice was ragged. 'When you are here, looking at me that way...'

'How can I help it?' He took her face between his long hands and kissed her lips tenderly. Then, as though making a promise, 'You shall have time to think. But don't keep me waiting too long.'

CHAPTER FOUR

TRUE to his word, Armand gave Claudie the time and space she had asked for in order to make her decision.

Perversely, it was somewhat upsetting to be taken quite so literally, when the subject had absorbed her thoughts and dreams almost exclusively.

A proposal of marriage was a momentous occasion at any time, but coming out of the blue and from a man who was virtually a stranger it could be anticipated to create a stir in anyone's life.

But not so, apparently, in the life of Armand Delacroix. For him, it seemed, it was business as usual.

In the days that followed, Claudie saw him only at a distance, as she explored the estate, and each time, it seemed, he was with Miranda Belling. Which was perfectly logical, of course. Miranda was, after all, his secretary. But seeing Miranda's glowing face as they passed her one afternoon, in a gleaming open sports car, Claudie guessed that the girl, at least, had her mind on something other than work.

Claudie had been sketching a delightful little copse from her vantage point on a dry stone wall when the car came jaunting along the narrow road. It drew to a halt some yards ahead and reversed back to where she was sitting.

'Is there anything you want from the town?' He had an extra layer of suntan which seemed to make the dark eyes sparkle. 'We will be back well in time for dinner.'

The 'we' cut Claudie to the quick. 'No, thanks.'

She kept her eyes down in pretended absorption in her sketch, until curiosity drove them to look up. The impact of his looks was as strong as the first time and it seemed incredible to believe this fantastic man had asked her to marry him. Perhaps she had dreamt it after all.

At the moment, he seemed perfectly content with his current companion. The bitter thought was a knife-twist in her heart.

In an ivory short-sleeved shirt and light brown trousers, he looked sensational. His hands were on the steering-wheel and her eyes were drawn to the dark hairs on his strong forearms.

Repressing a responsive shudder, she looked away and met his gaze, which held a gleam of humorous understanding.

Her teeth gripped her bottom lip in suppressed fury and it didn't improve her temper to notice the smile of triumph Miranda Belling wore like a banner.

Let her enjoy her moment, Claudie thought moodily. Tomorrow, it will probably be the maid's turn. That little spurt of venom revived her spirits.

'Good of you to ask,' she muttered finally. 'But I think I'm OK.'

'Another time, perhaps,' Miranda suggested in sweet condescension. 'Don't hesitate to ask.'

'Thanks.' Claudie's mouth tightened. She knew her annoyance was showing, but seemed unable to do anything about it.

Why was she annoyed anyway? she asked herself irritably after they'd driven away. She'd as good as turned him down, hadn't she? She could hardly complain if he'd taken advantage of other distractions offered. But he'd promised to wait until she'd made up her mind, her inner voice cried.

'What's the difference?' she derided herself aloud. 'You were going to say no anyway.'

Was she? Of course she was! It was the only sensible answer. But at the moment she didn't feel at all sensible... only hurt.

The track was very dry and the cloud of dust Armand's car had left behind still hung in the air, as thick as her confusion. She brushed ineffectually at the dancing motes as though brushing the angry thoughts from her mind. It wasn't as though she was the smallest bit interested in Armand Delacroix. His effect was entirely chemical and all she had to do was make sure no sparks leaped across to engage with her heart.

But that, it seemed, was easier said than done, and eventually she gave up her attempt at concentration and went home.

In the cool of the evening, he turned up unexpectedly on her doorstep.

'Oh! Hello!' she greeted him a little breathlessly, trying to still the erratic clamour of her heartbeat.

'You look startled,' he said with an ironic quirk of his mouth. 'Were you expecting someone else?'

'No. I just wasn't expecting anybody.' Claudie felt the colour rising into her cheeks as he bent to kiss her. 'Come in, please.'

He followed her into the bright salon, the tingle of his vitality reaching her even though he walked behind.

With a quick, nervous gesture she brushed the pale, silky curtain of hair back behind her ears. Had he come for his answer? 'Can I get you some coffee?'

He nodded. 'In a little while. But for now——' he patted the seat beside him '—spare a moment to relax.'

Claudie eyed him warily, thrown into immediate conflict by his gesture. She would have preferred to sit in the armchair some distance from the sofa, but to do so might seem pointedly rude. On the other hand, his nearness seemed something that was best avoided.

After her disastrous lack of control at their last meeting, she had every intention of keeping him at a distance—for her own peace of mind.

In the end, she sat on the sofa, keeping some little distance from him.

He raised dark eyebrows. 'Perhaps I should have thought to bring Madame Sicre, as chaperon.'

Claudie flushed at this evidence that he'd understood her gesture. 'Perhaps you should have,' she said, letting her irritation show. 'Why have you come?'

His eyes widened at her brusque approach, his gaze sweeping searchingly over her tense face for long, agonising moments that had Claudie's nerves stretched to the limit.

I'm not ready for this, she thought with a spurt of surprise which became panic as she realised she hadn't any decisive answer to give him. The battle between head and heart was still going on.

'I come with an invitation to a feast and later to a ball.'

His calm voice cut into her chaotic thoughts with the precision of a knife. Whatever else, she hadn't expected this.

'French country-style, of course,' he went on, as though the tension thick in the air between them didn't exist. 'To take place in the hall at the rear of the village school. Casual and a little homespun, but a good introduction for you into the local social scene. I think you might enjoy it.'

Claudie's mouth, which had been hanging open, snapped shut. She swallowed thickly several times before she could speak.

'How thoughtful. But actually, I don't think I'm proficient enough yet to risk my French in public.'

'You have to start somewhere,' he insisted, his dark eyes kindling with a spark of impatience. 'And I shall be there at your side to translate, if you get into difficulties.'

Claudie's heart bumped unevenly at this vision both tempting and terrifying. Then, gradually, it dawned on her that she had been offered a reprieve. The thing to do was keep the conversation cool and even.

'Oh, but I wouldn't want to monopolise your evening.' Despite everything, there was a faint stirring of excitement building up inside her. 'Wouldn't you prefer to be with your friends?'

His lip curled in amusement. 'Most of my time has been spent in Paris. My friends are there. Here in the country, I shall be as glad of your company as you may be of mine.'

Claudie had recovered sufficiently to wonder why he hadn't asked Miranda. But perhaps it wasn't *de rigueur* for a man in his position to appear at a public function with his secretary.

He said unexpectedly, his tone low and enticing, 'Come, Claudie! Too much solitude is bad. You would like a little company, wouldn't you?'

She nodded unwillingly. 'If that is all you're asking.'

He nodded. 'It's a place to begin.'

She met his gaze hesitantly and was startled by the light that burned there...the same point at which they'd met briefly once before, but now infinitely more penetrating and full of a strange intimacy. He seemed to be exploring the depths of her, searching for something she only vaguely understood, that awareness slipping away almost before it registered.

He reached out a hand and, in a daze, she took it. Imperceptibly, he moved closer, until Claudie was caught in his aura, feeling the vibrancy of his vitality as a magnetic force which seemed to draw her heart up into her throat, where she felt the urgency of its beat. He was too close for comfort and Claudie wished she could draw away, but it was too late.

He lowered his head, almost in slow motion, bringing his mouth close to hers, where she felt the sweet warmth of his breath against her lips. Lips that burned fiercely in anticipation of his kiss.

Mesmerised, her eyes held his, and she saw him smile…a soft, sensual movement of that alluring mouth, before it made contact with her own.

The kiss was over in a second, but seemed to have left an indelible impression on the petal softness of her mouth.

'So. You will come, *chérie*?' he murmured, moving back a little to look into her flushed face.

She nodded, unable, for the moment, to trust her voice.

He kissed her cheek. 'Then I shall come for you on Saturday at eight-thirty.'

'Yes.' The one stark word sounded inadequate measured against the searing moments that had just passed between them.

When he'd gone, she sat for some time, in a kind of daze, wondering where her willpower had gone. She'd promised herself she would remain aloof from him, to resist the charm she knew he was capable of exerting, and yet at the first hurdle she had wavered and fallen.

Annelise had hinted at his almost magic charm, but Claudie thought now that even she could not have known the full extent of his power.

But no ground had been lost that couldn't be recovered, she thought a little desperately.

When he'd kissed her goodbye, it had been on both cheeks, with no hint of anything other than courtesy. His *au revoir* was clipped and Claudie thought it possible that he was already regretting, as much as she, those moments of intimacy.

Saturday now loomed ahead, bringing a mixture of dread and painful anticipation.

She wondered if Miranda would be there and what her reaction would be to Claudie being escorted exclusively, as he had seemed to promise, by Armand Delacroix.

But in the event, Claudie saw Armand before then.

She slept badly and woke early and it seemed useless to go on lying in bed.

She got up, promising herself she would occupy the day usefully by beginning on the portfolio of designs Armand had suggested, but the world outside her front door was one of early morning enchantment. The dewy softness of the light made the grass look lush and green, the trees radiant in their full-leafed splendour, enticing her out of doors with her camera.

She took her camera and walked across the field to the rear of her house, heading upwards towards the top of a hill that would give her a good vantage point from which to take photographs.

Almost at the top, she stopped to rest and take a look at the view. It was breathtaking, with chequered fields of lush green, bright yellow and rich umber interspersed by the mottled blue green of pines rising up towards rocky outcrops.

Through the eye of the lens, she saw the horseman. Proud and still on a rocky outcrop. At this distance, his features were indistinct, but the regal bearing, the

arrogant tilt of the head, left her in no doubt that it was
Armand Delacroix.

The unexpected sight of him had her heart racing.
Despite the mixture of feelings he engendered in her,
there was still no denying the effect his looks had on her
senses.

She angled the camera once more. Inexplicably, her
fingers were shaky as she clicked the shutter, and she
gave an exasperated sigh. That shot had probably been
muzzy—a waste of good film. She would just have to
wait until the disturbing Frenchman had moved on before
taking another. Turning determinedly away, she continued to climb, reaching the summit a little out of
breath.

As she'd anticipated, the sun was growing hotter and,
removing the loose shirt she wore over her T-shirt, she
put it down on the ground beneath a tree, sitting down
on it to rest and cool off. Unable to resist the urge, she
scanned the expanse of grey rock on which she'd seen
Armand, but he was gone. A little stab of disappointment caught her by surprise and the place around
seemed suddenly empty. For Pete's sake, she thought
irritably, had she *wanted* him to be there?

A noise distracted her from her thoughts. A thin,
pitiful sound that pierced the silence and made her scalp
prickle with alarm. Some small animal, perhaps, in the
throes of mating fervour, she thought hopefully. But as
it came again and again, the sound becoming almost
human, she recognised a note of distress and got up to
investigate.

A narrow, dusty path led into the wood and she followed it slowly, trying to judge the direction of the sound.
It came again, louder, more urgent and she moved
quickly forward, crying out at the sight of the little dog,
crouched down on its haunches and, in between cries,

tugging frantically at something that held prisoner one of its front paws.

'Oh. You poor thing.' She knelt down beside the dog, which was some kind of small terrier. It looked up at her with bulging, frightened eyes and whimpered.

'All right, all right,' she soothed, touching its head reassuringly. 'Stay still and let me see if I can help you.'

The thing it had been tugging was a thin wire that was caught tightly around its right front paw. The dog's frantic tugging had only drawn the bond tighter and blood gushed from a wound which bit down to the bone.

Anger followed sharply on pity. The wire was a primitive snare in the form of a noose cruelly designed so that the more a creature struggled to be free, the tighter it would be held.

Gingerly, she lifted the dog, dropping it hurriedly as it snarled and snapped at the hand with which she was trying to loosen the noose. It obviously wasn't going to allow her to help it that way, she thought, fighting down a rising panic as the little dog struggled harder for freedom, causing the wire to bite deeper. Her interference was only making matters worse. And yet she couldn't just leave the poor little thing alone while she went for help.

The crying was upsetting her. She would have to think of something. Searching in the undergrowth, she found the peg which was holding the wire, but the stout piece of wood had been knocked deep into the ground and resisted all her efforts to pull it free.

Sweating and near to panic, she looked around, searching for something to knock it out, or at least loosen it, and picked up a heavy section of branch. She was wielding it, cursing the weakness of her muscles, when she was suddenly caught up from behind and pulled away.

'Claudie! Stop!' a deep voice said. 'Let me do it.'

She dropped the branch and turned into the strong arms which held her, burying her face against the hard-muscled chest for a few seconds before looking up into Armand's face, grim and pale beneath his tan. There was a film of sweat on his brow and, from the laboured breathing of his horse, tethered near by, he'd ridden hard.

A surge of relief filled her, followed by anger.

'Oh, yes! You do it! After all, it's you who is responsible for this.'

He said grimly, 'Calm down. Hysterics will help nobody.'

He put her from him and she stood back, panting with exertion and fury, watching as, with one strong movement of his arms, he yanked the peg free.

Claudie rushed forward to pick up the little dog, which was now lying limp and still.

For a moment, she hesitated, sickened by the sight of the wound and the blood, which seemed now to have stopped gushing. Then, with compassion overcoming her revulsion, she lifted the poor creature up, holding it against her, releasing the tumult of her feelings on to Armand, who was watching her, wiping the sweat from his forehead with the sleeve of his shirt.

'It's dead,' she said accusingly. 'Well, I hope you're satisfied.'

She was shaking, her nerves strung tight with shock and pity.

'It is not dead. Merely exhausted,' he said calmly, and commanded, 'Hold it still and I will try to remove this thing without causing more harm.'

To Claudie's relief, the little dog's eyes opened and it whimpered weakly as, with gentle hands, Armand worked the wire free. Blood was pouring anew from the wound, smearing his fingers and seeping up Claudie's arms to stain the sleeves of her T-shirt.

She was past caring. With tears of relief pressing behind her eyes, she cradled the little dog against her, crooning to it softly to comfort its trembling.

With a little tutting sound of impatience, Armand strode across to his horse and took the reins.

Claudie stared at him, her senses taking in the lithe vitality of him, the smears of blood on his arms and once immaculate shirt making it look as though he'd been engaged in some fierce male battle. Her stomach clenched, but it wasn't he who had sustained the wounds.

'Shining knight to the rescue,' she said, the resentful words spilling out. 'What would you have done if it had been a rabbit instead of a dog? Broken its neck and taken it home for the pot? I suppose you think that because that snare was intended for a wild creature instead of a domestic one, you can justify the barbarism.' She drew a trembling breath. 'I've heard about the Frenchman's disregard for animals, but I never thought——'

'Stop talking nonsense,' he ordered, impatiently cutting across her tirade and grasping her arm roughly. 'And get up on the horse. That poor creature needs the attentions of a *vetérinaire*. Or would your superior English brand of compassion allow him to bleed to death while you decide who is to blame for his misfortune?'

She bit hard on her lower lip, and allowed him to take the dog while she got up on to the tall roan. Nothing mattered now but to have the dog's wound attended to. Her views on cruelty to animals could wait for a more appropriate time.

Meanwhile, all she could do was pray it wouldn't die. Somebody, somewhere, must be worrying about the poor little thing.

'Whose dog is it? Do you know?' she asked, as Armand handed it up to her and climbed up behind, looping his arms about them both to take the reins.

'No. There are many such little dogs on the neighbouring farms. It could belong to anyone.'

Their journey to the nearest village was accomplished in a strangely taut silence. Claudie's anger had ebbed away, now they were engaged in positive action to help the little dog. Perhaps she had gone overboard a bit, she thought, wishing she could see his face to gauge his reaction to her barbed remarks. Why had she responded so strongly... so damningly?

Emerging from the surgery, carrying the sedated dog, Claudie felt a sense of anticlimax.

'What now?' She looked up at Armand questioningly. 'How do we go about finding his owner?'

'Word will get around and someone will come to claim him eventually,' Armand said, with a shrug. 'Until then, you must take him home with you and care for him.'

Claudie's jaw dropped. 'Me? Why me?'

One dark brow lifted ironically. 'It's the only solution, unless you wish to hand him over to a cruel and insensitive Frenchman.'

Claudie had the grace to colour. 'I... I'm sorry. I was angry. Cruelty in any form upsets me, but I still shouldn't have said what I did. I don't suppose Frenchmen care less for animals than anyone else.'

She cast him a sideways glance and found he was studying her intently, the dark eyes moving slowly over the planes of her face. She flushed and looked away, saying a little testily, 'Still. The snare was on your land, so you must accept some responsibility for the fact that it was there.'

He made a short sound of annoyance. 'It's impossible to guard the whole estate from poachers. Rabbits, deer, wild boar and even wild goats are hunted to fill bare tables. Since it's in the nature of culling and if it's kept within reasonable limits, I don't find that unacceptable. Snares I don't condone, but they're an unpleasant fact of life and unless I or a member of my staff actually catch someone laying them, there isn't much I can do about it, except get rid of them as and when we find them.'

Armand took the basket from her and helped her up on to the roan before handing it back. Then he mounted up behind her and took up the reins, turning the horse's head for home.

Even through her sweater, she felt the warm dampness of sweat on his shirt and remembered how he'd looked when he'd come on the scene.

'I'm glad you came when you did,' she said, by way of additional apology, relieved that he couldn't see the heat that was in her face from this close unnerving contact with him. 'You must have ridden quite hard to arrive so quickly. Could you hear the little dog crying from that distance?'

He said brusquely, 'I didn't know it was a dog. It might have been anything... anyone... perhaps even you.'

Claudie felt a little jolt of surprise. 'How did you know I was there?'

'The glint of the sun on your camera caught my attention,' he said, adding ironically, 'I have very good eyesight, and even at that distance you're hard to mistake for anyone else.'

'So are you.' A little gasp broke from her lips as she realised what she had given away. 'I... I saw you too. I was taking a photograph of the landscape and... you were there...'

'Yes. I was there.' He made an amused sound and Claudie felt its vibration tingling through her body, its

heat increasing as he went on in a voice that was deep
and mysterious, 'What is it that draws us together,
chérie? Fate or something else?'

'I don't know.' Her voice sounded husky and she
coughed, saying a little sharply to cover her embarrassment, 'Just plain coincidence, I suspect.'

He laughed shortly. 'Lucky coincidence, none the less.
Since I was around when you needed me.'

'Not me,' she denied hastily. 'The little dog.'

He shrugged. 'I couldn't have known that at the time.
I thought it was you who might be in trouble.'

She said hesitantly, 'So, you came riding to my rescue?'

'Yes, of course.' His arm tightened a little about her.
'And I got nothing for my chivalry but anger and
accusation.'

'What were you hoping for?' she demanded, in mock
indignation.

He turned her chin, so that he could see her face. 'Only
that I would find you safe.'

Claudie's hand clenched on the basket as she turned
her head shyly away. She didn't dare go on looking at
him. The intensity of his expression touched something
inside her, making her shiver, and he drew her closer
against him.

She felt the hard wall of his chest against her back
and the tingling vitality of him enveloped her in an almost
painful awareness. By the time they reached her front
door, she was oddly reluctant to relinquish the contact.

They put the little dog, still sleeping, in a little nook
by the fireplace. Reaching into the breast pocket of his
shirt, Armand took out the tablets the vet had given him
and placed them on the mantelshelf.

'He must remain sedated for a while, in case he is
tempted to stand on his injured paw. You should give
him one of these tablets every four hours during the day.'

She looked at him doubtfully. 'I'm not sure I'd know how. Do you think he'll swallow them of his own free will?'

'No, but he will succumb to your persuasions eventually. It isn't too difficult.'

'Not to you, perhaps,' she said a little irritably. 'But I don't have any experience of sick animals.'

He laughed indulgently. 'Perhaps you would like me to return to administer the first tablet so that you will know how to do it?'

He brushed a careless hand against the pale silk of her hair.

Claudie wished she could have ignored the intimate gesture, but the shock of his touch vibrated through her like a shudder. She hoped her quaking wasn't visible.

'No, thanks,' she said hastily, avoiding the dark humour of his eyes and wondering in embarrassment if he thought she had been angling for him to return. 'I'm sure I'll cope somehow.'

'Always so independent,' he said, his voice unexpectedly soft.

He was too near, she realised in dismay, as he continued to look down at her, studying her flushed face with that strange intensity she found so uncomfortable. She could feel the warmth of his muscular body, smell the male scent of him. It made her giddy. She jerked nervously away from him, willing him to go, and sighed with relief as he gave the shrug that always seemed to presage the departure of a Frenchman. 'I must go. But I will be back soon to see how the invalid progresses. *Au revoir*!'

'*Au revoir*!' Claudie responded, lifting her face for the anticipated touch of his lips against her cheeks.

But instead, his mouth brushed hers in a warm, brief kiss and she found herself stifling the wish to prolong the pressure of his lips on hers.

His dark brows arched and there was a faint tantalising smile curving the corners of his fascinating mouth.

'Until later,' he murmured, and was gone before her heartbeat returned to normal.

She showered, putting her bloodstained clothes in to soak in the large sink in the marble-tiled utility-room. Changing into a white scoop-necked dress that hung coolly and loosely about her curves, she brushed her long hair dry in the warm air and plaited a white ribbon into it to keep it away from her face.

The house still vibrated with the electric vitality of Armand Delacroix. Her mind still reeled with pictures of his strong, dark, handsome face, and her body retained the tingling sensations of his nearness on the journey home, the security of his encircling arms to keep her safely on their shared mount.

She made coffee and took it out on to one corner of the balcony where a trellis of overhanging vines provided shelter from the sun. The air was heavy with warmth and the scent of roses. Lounging back in a garden chair, she closed her eyes at the sheer bliss of it, only to find her vision haunted again by that handsome, enigmatic face.

She blinked the images away and drank her coffee. There was only one way to make Armand Delacroix disappear and that was to immerse herself in some work.

She set determinedly to work on her portfolio and soon became absorbed.

She was brought out of her absorption by faint cries from the living-room. She remembered her little invalid and felt a sharp pang of guilt as she realised that she'd completely forgotten about the little creature. It was

struggling to sit up as she hurried into the living-room.
She went over and picked it up.

'You're not supposed to do that,' she chided it as it
lay in her arms, staring up at her warily, a faint growling
sound rumbling through its hard little body. She rocked
it like a baby, trying to reassure it, but it didn't like that
very much either and the rumbling grew louder.

'Oh, dear,' she sighed aloud. 'What do I do now?'

'You give it another tablet before it comes around too
fully and bites the hand that saved it.'

The deep, masculine voice speaking to her from behind
startled her into almost dropping the poor thing.

Spinning around, she faced Armand Delacroix, feeling
her heart bump unevenly as he smiled. 'I seem to have
arrived just in time.'

Relieved, she smiled back. 'You couldn't have timed
it better.'

'Well, at least my welcome is improving,' he said wryly,
and, taking the tablets from the mantel, he shook one
out into his palm. 'You hold him steady while I administer the medicine. It won't take long.'

With easy assurance, he opened the dog's jaw and
popped the tablet to the back of its tongue, holding its
mouth closed with one hand while massaging its throat
with the other. His eyes were lowered in concentration,
his head bent, close to hers. Claudie looked at the thick
dark fan of his lashes spread across his tanned cheeks
and felt a tremor pass through her.

There was no denying it, he was a very attractive man,
but it was the pull of his almost animal vitality that drew
her most strongly. This close, it was impossible not to
feel the heady flow of excitement, or to control the hectic
pulse that beat in her throat.

'There,' he said, straightening at last. 'He has
swallowed it. Now he will sleep.'

'Thank goodness!' Claudie exclaimed fervently. 'I just hope I don't have to get up in the middle of the night to give him the next pill?' She felt aghast at the idea that the invalid might bite if she left it too long in between doses.

He laughed. 'You won't. I have some good news for you. The owner is an elderly farmer on the other side of the village and I have offered to pick the dog up and return it to him.'

'Oh, I see.' Claudie's relief was tinged by something that felt like disappointment. 'So that's why you came back?'

'Yes. Of course.' He reached across for the basket. 'I think you should come with me. I am sure the farmer wishes to thank you personally for saving his little companion.'

'I didn't save him. You did,' she said drily. 'I wouldn't want to steal your glory.'

He said firmly, 'We'll share the glory. Come! I won't take no for an answer.'

'I know,' she agreed glumly, and went to fetch her jacket.

CHAPTER FIVE

THE farm was old and, although it looked in good condition from the outside, the inside was spartan. A huge kitchen with dark beams, grey paved floor and a shallow stone sink built into the wall like a grotto. An assortment of pots and pans, some gleaming copper, ranged about the walls, and a long wooden table, scarred and weathered, took up the whole of the central space, around which rickety chairs of different vintages were collected.

Claudie looked around in amazement. They might have been back in the Middle Ages. The old farmer was as thin as a whippet and when he smiled he revealed numerous gaps in his teeth.

He and his wife were quite obviously happy to have their missing pet returned.

'My French must be improving,' Claudie said to Armand as he drove the car home. 'I could understand practically all the old couple said.'

Armand laughed. 'That's because they were talking to you in baby French.'

'In baby French!' she repeated indignantly. 'Why on earth should they do that?'

His dark eyes danced with amusement. 'Because they wanted to speak to you personally, not through me, and they were making it easy for you.'

Claudie flushed, a little ashamed of her irritable reaction. 'That was very kind.'

'They weren't being kind,' he said drily. 'Just curious. When one speaks, one tells far more than one knows.'

She looked puzzled. 'But why should they be curious about me?'

He shrugged. 'Curiosity is part of human nature.'

They were back at her house and he drew the car to a halt, releasing his seatbelt and hers before meeting her irritated gaze.

'There are times,' Claudie said, 'when I despair of ever having a sensible conversation with you.'

He turned and put his hands on her shoulders, where they burned like brands.

His eyes looked deeply into hers. 'We speak a personal language, you and I, *chérie*,' he said softly. 'Different from the everyday. And I know that you understand.'

She shook her head. 'I don't. Oh, Armand, I don't.'

'Sweet liar!' he said and, cupping her face tenderly, he kissed her.

His mouth was firm and sweet on hers, the touch of his hands against her face strangely moving. She covered them with her fingers, feeling their gentle strength, the smooth hardness of the skin, the fine layer of hair, and made a sound that rose from somewhere deep inside.

As though it was the signal he was waiting for, he drew her into his arms and the kiss deepened to fiery intensity, exploring the contours of her mouth with his tongue, building an excitement that was difficult to contain. Almost wildly, her lips and tongue answered his. She strained towards him and he drew her tighter, crushing her possessively against his lithe body.

She felt his hands moving against her and she touched him in return, stroking over the hard muscle of his shoulders and chest, frustrated by the clothing that covered him. She undid the buttons of his shirt, sighing as her fingers made contact with his skin, and felt him shudder in response.

He took her hand then and brought it lower, pressing it against the hardness of him, and lifted his lips to murmur huskily, 'The message is silent but clear, sweet Claudie. You understood without a word being spoken.'

As though dashed with cold water, Claudie jerked away from him.

'Yes. I understood. You just want to get me into bed.'

He shook his head. 'Oh, *chérie*! How mundane you make that sound, when in reality it would be heaven.'

'Heaven! Perhaps! For a while, until someone new comes along.'

He frowned. 'When I make love to you, I will not be thinking of the last, nor the next, but only of how you make me feel and how I can make you feel.'

She said angrily, 'You are always so sure of your sex appeal, aren't you?'

He shrugged. 'We all have it in one degree or another. Why shouldn't I be aware of it?' He grimaced. 'But were we speaking of sex? Is that the message that you heard and responded to?'

Claudie's colour flared. 'I wasn't talking about myself, but about you. You! And all the women you've collected like scalps all your life.'

His expression changed from rueful to furious. 'What do you know of me, *petite Anglaise*? What you have heard at second hand? Gossip and speculation are no standards by which to judge the heart of a man.'

She said, 'Not even when he has no heart?'

But his anger had disappeared as swiftly as it had come.

'I have a heart, *chérie*. You felt its beat moments ago, with your hand hot against me. Here!' Before she could withdraw it, he'd taken her hand and placed it against his chest. The steady thudding of his heartbeat spread through her, joining rhythm with her own.

She gasped. 'Let me go.'

'No,' he said, tightening his hold on her wrist. 'I was tempted to let you go, but you see, I know your heart better than you know mine.'

His free hand touched her breast, pressed against the racing tumult he was creating. 'And your heart and mine are in accord, though you may deny it.'

She wanted desperately to pull away, to go on denying what was becoming ever more clear to both of them. But his gaze and the magic of his hand moving gently now and erotically against the hardening peak of her breast kept her still. She wanted him. God, how she wanted him! But not like this.

Her mouth trembled. 'Why do you want to humiliate me?'

He drew a sharp, exasperated breath. 'Are you telling me now that it is humiliating to be desired?'

'What is desire but lust?' Her voice was ragged with hurt.

'That's the nature of it, *chérie*. Attraction, lust, desire, love. Whatever the name, they are all one, leading to the meeting of two people in fulfilment.'

Claudie was mesmerised by the dark depths of his gaze, fixed intently on hers.

'And after that meeting? When it's over?' she questioned tremulously, because tears were very close.

'After that——' he traced a finger down her cheek to her lips '—there remains whatever two people wish. What do you wish?'

Her mouth tightened with the force of her frustration. 'You answer question with question, never with an answer.'

'One final question, then. Do you wish to marry me?'

She said harshly, 'What kind of question is that? Wishes are for things out of reach. Dreams.'

She had dreamt of him many times over the years...fantasised about a marriage to the French prince of her godmother's stories. Fairy-tale stuff...with no place in reality.

He said enticingly, 'Then have your dreams, *chérie*. And let me make them come true.'

Claudie recoiled, shaken by the pictures her mind was conjuring up. 'You promised you would give me time.'

He said impatiently, 'And haven't I given you time? God knows I've struggled hard with my impatience. But when we're together and I hold you like this, you give me your answer with your lips, with your body. Why won't you put it into words?' He gripped her arms fiercely and shook her a little. 'Claudie! Say yes!'

She stared at him, her large violet eyes wide with dismay.

It was unbearable that he was aware of the fires of passion that burned within her when she was in his arms. If she could but trust her own body to know the truth. If she could trust him!

But the past had been with her for longer than the present and it had taught her that for Armand Delacroix love was a game...and with the winning came disenchantment.

And yet still she couldn't say the one little word that would release her from the danger he represented.

No! The word echoed in her head, but would not form on her lips.

'I just can't,' she whispered, her voice broken by emotion.

He sighed deeply. 'Ah! *Chérie*!'

His strong arms closed about her gently, giving comfort that was very sweet, and his mouth lowered to hers in a soft kiss that made no demand.

A trickle of fear ran down Claudie's spine and a small voice rose to warn her. With gentleness as his weapon, he might still win the game.

At her front door, to which he'd escorted her in a daze, she spoke hesitantly.

'Do you still want to take me to the fête on Saturday?'

It was somehow very important that he should want to see her again soon.

'But of course.' He laughed and stroked her cheek with the back of his hand. 'Sleep well, *chérie*. And you will dream of me a little, *non*?'

He couldn't know she'd spent most of her life doing just that.

Saturday arrived at last and, despite the clouds drifting across the sun for most of the day, the evening sky was clear and the temperature warm.

Claudie had woken with a nervy, restless feeling and the day had seemed endless. She spent the time doing small tasks, because she couldn't concentrate long enough for anything else. Her mind was busy with the subject that occupied her endlessly in circular thinking. Armand's proposal.

By evening, she was a mass of nerves.

She dressed in a sleeveless, scoop-necked white dress, with a thin red leather belt, which made her look young and vexingly vulnerable, until she added the little scarlet bolero jacket. She painted her mouth with a matching lipstick and heightened her eye make-up to balance the bright colour and nodded her head in satisfaction. She still looked young, but perhaps not quite so green.

Armand seemed approving as he looked her over appraisingly at her doorstep.

Claudie flushed under his keen scrutiny, and did a little defiant appraising of her own, allowing her gaze to sweep

from his dark, handsome head to the casual but im-
maculately cut shirt and trousers and down to the ex-
pensive-looking, probably Italian, leather shoes.

At the end of this mutual inspection, he smiled. 'Well,
my opinion is that we make a beautiful couple.'

There was amusement in the deep, alluring voice, as
though he'd enjoyed rather than resented her chal-
lenging stare.

She was suddenly light-hearted. 'I'd just reached the
same conclusion myself.'

With the warm weather and its promise of a balmy
night, the tables had been laid out of doors instead of
in the school hall. Long wooden trestle tables had been
arranged as three sides of a square, covered in spotless
sheets of white linen and highlighted with porcelain vases
containing small bunches of wild flowers. Claudie was
delighted. Out here, in the open air, the atmosphere
seemed less formal . . . more friendly.

The faces that greeted them smiled a lot in seeming
welcome, but Claudie was glad of Armand's hand tucked
beneath her elbow as he led her around for the
introductions.

He allowed her to struggle with her French, only
coming to her rescue when she was really stuck. She shot
him a look of resentment, which he answered with the
lift of his brows and a bland smile.

There was obvious curiosity, as well as welcome, in
the smiles of greeting, but that was to be expected.

Claudie knew that the Delacroix family had been the
biggest landowners in the area for centuries. Rich and
respected, and probably envied, they and their affairs
would always capture the interest of the other inhabitants of the commune.

To her dismay, the mayor came across and drew
Armand aside. He kissed her hand with a little smile of

apology and said softly in English, 'One moment and I'll be back, I promise.'

Claudie felt a moment's panic, as she was left to struggle alone in the sea of strangers, but she wasn't alone for long.

'You're Claudie Drew, aren't you?'

A voice spoke in English with an oddly mixed accent that sounded faintly American.

'Yes.' Claudie turned, with relief, towards the fair girl at her elbow, who was appraising her with twinkling green eyes. 'How did you know?'

'Word gets around here. Fast.'

The girl held out her hand and Claudie shook it warmly.

'I'm Jacqueline Di Maio. My husband Frank's the local plumber. That's him over there.' She pointed to a tall dark-haired man standing near by with a group of men. 'Talking shop as usual.'

She nodded across to where Armand was deep in conversation with the mayor. 'Looks as if we're in the same boat for the moment.'

'Yes,' Claudie agreed. 'Left to sink or swim. And my French is terrible. How's yours?'

Jacqueline laughed. 'A little better, maybe. I'm French. I only *married* a foreigner. Frank's American. We met when I was over there, so I stayed awhile, long enough to get married. We've been back here about six years.'

'That explains the accent,' Claudie said, and they laughed.

'Looks as if you'll be staying around here too.' There was a faint gleam of mischief in the green eyes. 'I mean, since you and Armand get on so well together.'

'Yes. I'm staying.' Claudie flushed under the keen regard. 'But what makes you think Armand and I get on that well? We've only just met.'

She felt embarrassed. Was her glow obvious enough to be seen by others? she wondered.

'Well, apart from the fact that I've never seen him so animated in any other woman's company, there are other things that give his interest away.'

'Such as?' Claudie waited in unwilling anticipation.

'He's here with you tonight, isn't he? Letting you be vetted by the local dignitaries, not to mention the locals. My! That's got to mean he's serious and doesn't care who knows it. Why, it's almost as good as a public declaration of intent.'

Claudie's insides churned uncomfortably. Had that been his intention? To put her in a position where she dared not refuse him without embarrassment? Was it possible he really was determined to marry her?

Of course not. She derided herself for the surge of hope that suddenly filled her. Americans were known to be dramatic. Add to that the notorious French curiosity...

'In England that wouldn't mean a thing,' she said a little stiffly.

Jacqueline gave her a sly smile. 'But this is France, where it does. Do you mean he hasn't already made a pass at you?'

'No.' Claudie crossed her fingers behind her back, feeling the lie was justified. 'So you can all stop speculating.'

Jacqueline's expression turned dreamy. 'But he's dishy, isn't he? If I wasn't happily married...' She let the words tail off and sighed.

Claudie said grudgingly, 'He's good-looking, I admit.'

'Oh, come on!' Jacqueline laughed. 'Don't be coy! Enjoy your luck! All the single women here, and some of the married ones too, I guess, would give their eye-teeth to be in your shoes. And that was even before the will.'

A shadow loomed suddenly.

'Madame Di Maio. How pleasant to see you.'

Armand was back, as he'd promised. He spoke in French, and saluted Jacqueline with a brief kiss on both cheeks. He was smiling, but Claudie was surprised by the coldness of his eyes.

Jacqueline saw it too and seemed flustered. She answered him in English.

'Just saying hello to Claudie. It's real nice to have the chance to speak English. Frank doesn't any more.'

'I'm sure. Give Frank my regards, though we're sure to meet later. *Au revoir*!'

He took Claudie's elbow and said a little abruptly, 'I think the meal's about to begin.'

Claudie hardly had time to wave at her new-found friend before he whisked her away. She had a brief second to wonder why Armand seemed to like Jacqueline Di Maio less than Claudie did.

The meal was a long-drawn-out affair, with course after course of food, which disappeared as before a swarm of locusts.

Armand relaxed as the evening wore on and the wine flowed. In response to his easy charm, Claudie felt herself letting go of the tension that had been building up in her all day.

They sat side by side, shoulders touching occasionally as he leaned over to amuse her with wry tales of the ancient scandals and feuds involving ancestors of the families represented there. Claudie felt herself being drawn more and more into the magic of his personality.

Smiling up into his devastatingly handsome face, she was aware of a warm, melting sensation that had nothing to do with the wine she was sipping. No wonder the women in the region had their eyes on him. What female wouldn't? He was the most fascinating man here, by any standards.

She frowned, remembering something Jacqueline had said. But what did the will have to do with Armand's fatal attractions? Would he be amused if she asked? She decided he wouldn't, and she didn't want to spoil the easy rapport that had been building up between them all evening.

At last, the food was cleared away and the tiny cups of coffee brought and drunk and the dancing began. A large area of grass had been covered with smooth boards and a canvas canopy erected above. With none of the usual hesitancy, the waiting for others to lead the way, eager dancers converged on the floor.

Claudie watched them in fascination. Round and round they spun, like gaily coloured tops, waltzing to the catchy, if somewhat repetitious, music. When the tune stopped, nobody seemed to leave the floor. They stood around in laughing groups waiting for the next.

'They're very enthusiastic, aren't they?' she commented in surprise.

Armand laughed. 'In the country, folk have to take their pleasures where they find them. They work hard and it would be a dull life otherwise.'

Claudie looked up at him curiously. 'Do you find the countryside dull after life in Paris?'

He shrugged. 'Not for the amount of time I need to spend here.'

She said in surprise, 'So you don't intend to live permanently at St Julien and run the estate?'

His handsome face closed suddenly. 'It depends on how things work out. The estate managers cope well enough without me and I have a business of my own in Paris.'

She felt oddly disappointed and a little depressed, though it was difficult to know why. But it seemed that, even if she did agree to marry him, it would make little difference to his lifestyle.

'Would you like to dance?' Taking her hand, Armand stood up, but she hesitated.

'I haven't waltzed since school.'

He smiled mockingly down at her, little laughter-lines appearing at the corners of his dark eyes. 'Not so long that you can have forgotten, then.' His strong hand hooked about her waist as he led her forward, and her trembling wasn't all nervousness about her dancing.

People parted to make space for them on the floor and Claudie saw the little nudges they gave each other as he took her in his arms.

'Are people here always so interested in what you do?' she asked him, feeling self-conscious.

'Always,' he said gravely, but with a gleam of humour in his dark eyes.

Despite her reservations, Claudie floated like a cloud within the circle of his arms. He held her firmly, but not too tightly, and together they whirled with the rest, until she was breathless.

'Have you had enough?' he asked at last.

'I think so.'

She felt strange now the momentum had stopped and staggered a little as he released her. He put his arm back about her waist, holding her firmly to his side as he cleared a way through the crowd. As the warmth of his hand penetrated the thin material of her dress, spears of sensation shot up Claudie's spine and she half closed her eyes to catch her breath.

'One twirl too many?' he enquired, looking down at her with a teasing glint in his eyes.

She nodded and then put a hand to her dizzy head. 'Or one glass of wine too many.'

'One less and you'd have had none,' he laughed, and led her away from the group crowded around the dance-floor.

It was dark now, Claudie realised with surprise. The time had passed so quickly that she hadn't noticed the transition from dusk. Coloured bulbs, strung out in the trees, cast little pools of light round about.

They sat on a rough wooden bench beneath the trees and breathed in the warm, scented air.

'I shouldn't have danced so soon after that huge meal,' she said with a sigh. 'Not that I ate a fraction of what everyone else seemed able to manage.'

He smiled. 'We French eat well, *non*?'

'Goodness, yes!' Claudie exclaimed laughingly. 'I'm amazed you aren't all huge.'

His eyes danced with unexpected mischief. 'Perhaps we burn off the calories in nervous energy.'

There was something intimate in the tone of his voice that made her own nerves tingle.

'I wouldn't say you were nervous,' she said, sounding strangely husky. 'Are you?'

He shrugged and spread his hands. 'Perhaps, a little, when I'm with a really beautiful woman.'

She looked into his mocking eyes and said, after a strangely charged silence, 'Then you must be nervous often.'

His expression changed, the indentations in his cheek deepening, his brows lowering. The dark frown only seemed to add to his attraction, making Claudie's pulse race with more than apprehension.

'That's the second time you've mentioned other women. Do you really imagine I have had that many?'

She bit her lip, feeling the heat burning in her cheeks. 'I don't know. But your reputation...'

He waved an irritable hand, bringing her to a halt, and his eyes narrowed assessingly on her flushed face. Claudie found she was holding her breath and wished she hadn't let her tongue run away with her.

He said, 'Reputations, especially bad ones, grow from the tiniest seeds, *chérie*. You would do better to trust your own judgement.'

Claudie lowered her head, finding it impossible to reply.

The voice of Annelise rose from the past to haunt her.

'Ah! These women! They spoil my wicked Armand,' she'd lamented. 'He's so blasé, I despair of him ever finding one to whom he can remain faithful.'

Very young and dreamy-eyed... full of her fantasies, hardly knowing the import of the words, Claudie had whispered softly, 'Oh, but he would be faithful to me.'

She groaned as she remembered her childhood boast, and put her hand to her head.

'Still giddy?' Armand enquired, a surprisingly soft note in his deep voice.

'A little.' Claudie was glad of the excuse he offered.

She was startled to feel his arm slide about her shoulders.

'Rest your head here, if you wish,' he said, tapping his upper arm invitingly. 'Until you feel better.'

As she looked at the broad, muscular shoulders, the somehow erotic strength of his neck, Claudie's mouth was suddenly dry. She sat up a little straighter. 'Thanks. But I'm fine.'

'Ah. The stiff upper lip of the English. It will carry you through, *non*? So independent,' he mocked, gently cupping her cheek to turn her face to his. 'Yet sometimes it is good to yield.'

'Yield to what?' Her voice shook.

She tried to read his eyes, dark pools, reflecting pinpoints of coloured lights as they gazed into hers.

'The answer to that you must find in your heart, *chérie*.'

The planes of his face were shadowed and mysterious as he went on searching her eyes.

Now! she thought. Now, he is going to ask me again. But the scales in her mind had tipped once more out of balance. Don't ask me now, she begged.

Almost abruptly, as though he'd heard her silent plea, he took his arm away.

'If you reject comfort, then perhaps a drink.'

'I think I've had enough alcohol already,' Claudie protested.

'Lemonade or fruit juice, then?'

'That would be nice.' Claudie was having trouble swallowing back a strange lump that had risen in her throat. 'Yes. A pineapple juice if there is one.'

She drew a deep breath as he went off across the grass to the long table now laid with drinks. The evening had been a strange but happy one, with Armand, as a confusingly gentle escort, even more of an enigma than before. Was she really as special as he was making her feel?

'Enjoying yourself, Miss Drew?'

Claudie came to with a start to find herself looking up into Miranda Belling's cool and beautiful face.

'Yes. Very much.' Claudie tried to match the coolness.

Miranda sat beside her. 'Good. Then I take it Armand is performing well in his role of gracious host.' Her laugh was a little offbeat. 'He does it well, doesn't he?'

'Charmingly.' Claudie's smile felt as though it had been pasted on, but she was determined not to let Miranda's taunts get under her skin. 'I didn't see you earlier, at the meal. Did you miss it?'

Some painful emotion flitted across the girl's features, to be banished by that cool smile.

'Unfortunately yes.' She gave a coy little laugh that went oddly with her strained expression. 'Armand was so disappointed when I told him I couldn't make it in time.' Her mouth curled. 'Still, I imagine he managed to pass the time pleasantly enough.'

Claudie wanted to tell her just how pleasant the evening had been and some small inner devil tempted her, just for the pleasure of seeing that smile washed off the girl's face, to reveal that Armand had proposed. But some small vestige of common sense kept her tongue still, contenting herself with a sweet barbed smile that was really foreign to her nature.

'Thank you, yes. We enjoyed ourselves very much. Such a pity you couldn't have been there.'

'Yes, wasn't it?' Miranda stood up. 'I really must go and find Armand. He'll be so pleased to know I've finally arrived.'

Claudie felt again that peculiar churning sensation in her stomach as she watched Miranda cross to the drinks table, where Armand was just about to lift two glasses.

He put his hands on Miranda's arms as she kissed him on both cheeks, looking down intently into her face as she spoke to him, a wide smile curving her mouth. He smiled back, looking pleased, and she took his hand in hers, trying to lead him away. He shook his head and came swiftly across to Claudie, a pineapple juice in his hand.

'Please forgive me! Something has occurred that needs my urgent attention. I will return as soon as I can.'

Trying hard not to feel angry, she sat for quite some time, hoping he would come back quickly. Was it her imagination, or were curious eyes casting furtive glances in her direction, sitting alone without Armand?

When, after what seemed an age, he didn't return, she stood up, looking around irresolutely before finally moving into the shadows, making her way around on the far side of the field, away from the lights and the music and the crowds. She followed the pathway that led around the side of the schoolhouse and found herself on the road that led homewards. Her house was only two kilometres or so away, within easy walking distance during the day, but here, away from the lighted windows of the school, the night was almost pitch dark, the thin moon barely shedding a light.

For a moment she was tempted to try for it anyway, even if she ended up crawling to find her way in the dark, but common sense prevailed and she stood trying to find an explanation for the dreadful fury that was tearing her apart. After all, what had happened? Her escort—for, despite his unanswered proposal, that was all Armand Delacroix was—had taken a little time off to dance with somebody else. Hardly cause for a melo-dramatic exit. She was behaving like a fool.

Slowly the fury drained away to be replaced by em-barrassment. How many eyes had witnessed her de-parture? And how would she ever have explained it to Armand if she had actually gone?

CHAPTER SIX

TAKING a deep breath to steel herself, Claudie began to walk as casually as she could manage around the side of the schoolhouse, making her way back towards the dance-floor, where couples were still merrily twirling away.

She saw her red bolero draped about the back of one of the chairs and went to fetch it, feeling a little spurt of relief. Here was her excuse for her absence, if she should need one.

The bench beneath the trees was still empty, she noted, with a stab of renewed fury, hastily subdued. This way, at least, he need never know she'd gone.

'All alone, *ma belle*,' someone said softly in French.

Claudie started nervously as a tall, slim figure slipped into her path. She let out a sigh of relief when she saw it was Pascal.

'Oh! It's you, Pascal!' she said slowly, trying to re-capture her wits. 'Yes. Armand has…er…' She ground to a halt, unable through the tumult of her feelings to think of a suitable excuse.

'Left for pastures new?' Pascal slipped his arm through hers. 'I understand.' He said it kindly. 'And, in time, you will too. For Armand, one woman is never enough.'

Claudie frowned to hide her humiliation. 'Your cousin and I are simply acquaintances. I don't expect him to remain glued to my side for the whole evening.'

'Ah! *Non*!' Pascal grinned, looking boyish with delight. 'And by the same token, you are also free to please yourself.'

'Of course.' Claudie's answering smile was stiff.

'Then come! Let's dance.'

Still clutching her bolero, she let him lead her back to the dance-floor. She dropped it on to a chair as she paused, relieved now to be swept along by Pascal's enthusiasm.

The music had changed to a slow, modern rhythm and there were fewer people dancing, now mainly younger couples holding each other close.

Pascal drew her into his arms, overcoming her small initial resistance, to place his cheek against her temple. With a little sigh she relaxed against him, suddenly glad of his moral support.

But when his lips brushed the side of her temple she pulled away a little. His nearness brought a strange uneasiness, unlike the pulsing excitement of Armand's presence.

'Pascal,' she said, making conversation an excuse for her withdrawal, but also because she needed to satisfy her curiosity, 'what was this riddle you were going to help me solve?'

He smiled an odd little smile. 'Hasn't it begun to unravel itself yet?'

Claudie frowned. 'No. Has it anything to do with Annelise's will?'

'Yes. But mainly it has to do with Armand, and you have forbidden me to speak of him.'

She sighed impatiently. 'If it's part of your fight with him, then I'd rather not hear.'

'Closing your ears and eyes to the truth, particularly where Armand is concerned, could be dangerous.'

'The real truth?' she demanded heatedly. 'Or your version?'

'Ah! Claudie!' He gave her a sorrowful look. 'Are you falling already under his spell as Annelise had hoped?'

'What...what do you mean?' The words were thick in her throat as she felt the tension in him.

'Annelise left you to Armand in her will, along with his inheritance. If he refuses to take you, he loses the rest.'

She stopped moving and stared up at him. 'Annelise named me as a bequest to Armand in her will?'

'*Non, non, non*!' he said ironically. 'My revered aunt was a little more subtle than that. She stipulated that he must marry a "local" girl within one month of the reading of the will or lose everything. Then, with her usual cunning, she placed you very temptingly on his doorstep.'

Claudie felt her knees begin to buckle. 'But that's ridiculous. Even if what you say were true, it doesn't have to be me. He could choose anyone.'

Pascal laughed sharply. 'Have you taken a look at the real local girls here in the heart of the countryside? Farmers' daughters mostly, hardly sophisticated enough for my dear cousin, as Annelise would know.'

'But...' Claudie's mind cast around wildly. 'There's Miranda.'

'All Miranda has to offer has been explored already by my cousin. She has no longer the power to hold him faithful. Such a situation for Armand would be a trial beyond bearing,' Pascal said in cool amusement.

Bent on malice, he failed to notice that his casual confirmation of her suspicions had cut Claudie to the quick, and he went on unheeding.

'Your innocent beauty is a far more enticing proposition for someone as jaded as Armand. With you as his wife, it is possible he might manage to curb his base nature and stay faithful for one year.' He laughed. 'Another of Annelise's teasing little stipulations.'

'But why on earth...?' She stopped, at a loss for words.

'Who knows?' Pascal shrugged. 'An optimistic hope, perhaps, that after a year of enforced fidelity it might become a habit.'

It was unbelievable that Annelise's fear—that Armand might never marry and give love a chance—had driven her to these curious lengths. But, deny it though she might, it all fell horribly into place.

Claudie's mouth was so dry she could barely manage to swallow. Hadn't Armand himself claimed her as part of Annelise's bequest? Other memories surfaced. Armand's granite-hard face telling her no one would ever take from him his inheritance. And he had asked her to marry him almost immediately, hadn't he?

'And if he doesn't...marry...and...?' Her voice caught in her throat.

'And stay faithful for one year?' Pascal prompted in gleeful malice. 'He loses everything to the despised stepson of her least favourite brother.' He straightened and drew up his chest. 'In other words, to me!'

Nauseous with shock, Claudie could bear no longer to stay there on the dance-floor, going through the social motions, when every part of her was in danger of collapse.

'My cousin has already proposed, has he not?' Pascal's voice was full of sudden tension.

Unable to find the energy to lie, Claudie nodded.

Pascal nodded too. 'An action I was anticipating from the moment I set eyes on you. He would have been relieved to know he was so lucky.'

Her dazed eyes met his. 'Lucky? I don't understand. In what way?'

His laugh was brittle. 'If you had been very ugly, he would still have married you and would have had a great struggle for a year. But with your beauty, even he would not easily grow tired and he would have much less trouble fulfilling the terms of the will by remaining faithful.'

Cold and empty inside, Claudie said through stiff lips, 'Even if I *were* ugly, I wouldn't marry him.'

'So! You have not accepted him?' Pascal's voice was triumphant.

'No. Of course not.' She knew suddenly that it was true. 'When I marry it will be for love. And I do not love Armand Delacroix.' She said it like an incantation, warding off the threat of evil.

'How perceptive of you, *ma belle*: to have seen Armand as he really is.' Pascal's cheek rested against her temple, his words murmuring through her hair, little darts of poison adroitly finding their mark. 'It is not in his nature to be faithful, not even to one as lovely as you. It is only the chase that he loves. It is never long before he discards one woman in favour of another.'

In her heart, Claudie knew it was true. As attentive and charming as Armand had been to her tonight, and despite what Pascal had said about Miranda's lack of appeal, it had taken very little effort on the part of his secretary to distract him away.

'I think I would like to sit down,' she said weakly.

When they came off the floor, Armand was there, his narrowed eyes watching their approach. He greeted Pascal in a cold voice.

'I had not thought to see you tonight. Your business venture was a success, I hope.'

'More successful than even *I'd* hoped.' Pascal sounded triumphant.

'Good! Then we'll leave you to enjoy the remainder of the evening.'

To Claudie he said, 'It was unfortunate that I was called away to attend to an urgent matter.' He took her arm to draw her to his side, away from Pascal. 'But that doesn't excuse my rudeness. Forgive me.'

Forgive him! She didn't think she ever would.

'There was no need for you to have rushed,' she said with ringing sarcasm. 'I've had a wonderful time... dancing with Pascal and... getting to know him.'

'I doubt if you would have continued to enjoy the experience,' he said, thin-lipped. 'Now, if you're ready to leave?'

Pascal was still there beside them, taking obvious delight in the knowledge that his presence infuriated Armand.

On a false note of concern, he said tauntingly, 'At your age, dear cousin, it is understandable that you are tired.' He reached out suddenly to take Claudie's hand. 'But Claudie and I are as young as the night.' He kissed her icy fingers. 'Will you stay and dance with me into the dawn?'

Armand gave a short derisive laugh. 'It seems you may have missed your vocation, Pascal. Instead of painting, you should be writing poetry.' His eyes narrowed in a hard stare. 'But perhaps that wouldn't pay quite so well as your art.'

'It could hardly pay less,' Pascal replied harshly. 'But perhaps soon I shall not have to worry about money.'

'*Oui*?' Armand's dark brows rose, a contemptuous question. 'Then, have you at last produced a masterpiece? Bravo!'

Ignoring the ugly look Pascal sent him, he walked to the chair on to which Claudie had tossed her jacket and came back, holding it out to her.

'Come, *mademoiselle*. As enticing as my cousin's invitation may be, I'll sleep more soundly knowing that it was I who saw you safely to your door.'

Claudie stood poised between the two men, too confused and weary even for anger.

Pascal's eyes on hers seemed malevolent. 'Armand doesn't own you, Claudie, however much he may wish to. Stay with me.'

'Thanks,' she managed through lips she could scarcely move. 'But I really am too tired to go on dancing tonight.'

Pascal's smile was thin, his eyes not on Claudie, but looking over her head into Armand's inscrutable face.

'There will be other times for us, *ma belle*,' he said. 'You may be sure of that.'

In the car, on the way home, Claudie sat beside Armand in the silence that neither seemed inclined to break, until they had reached her door.

'I won't ask you in for coffee,' she said in a tight voice.

He said, 'I will come in, none the less.'

Despite her hand holding the door to bar his way, he entered and turned to face her.

'Claudie, my sudden disappearance this evening must have upset you. That is natural.' He took her cold hand in his strong, warm fingers and squeezed it. 'But, some time soon, I will explain.'

'There isn't any need,' she said, withdrawing her hand forcefully from his. She wanted to cry. 'I'm glad I was able to fill in until Miranda arrived. At least your evening wasn't entirely wasted.'

He stared at her for some seconds and then, taking her cue, he said brightly, 'Oh, no. Not *entirely* wasted. I've learned one or two things worth knowing.'

'So have I.' Claudie's temper suddenly took over from her inexplicable pain. 'And I wouldn't marry you if you begged me a thousand times.'

To her furious surprise, he laughed, and she flung herself at him, beating at his chest with her fists, before he captured them in his hands.

'Oh, Claudie! Such fiery passion! I wish it were of another kind.' He laughed and said softly, 'And all because of a little time spent alone without an explanation? Sometimes you are such a child.'

He released her wrists, but before she could stop him he'd pulled her roughly into his arms, crushing her protests with his mouth, maintaining the hard pressure until her struggles ceased.

Then, as her strength waned, he kissed her, deeply and thoroughly, until she was clinging to him for support against her own weakness.

Then, ever so gently, he disentangled her from him and pushed her away.

'I must go. Sleep well, *chérie*.'

Claudie tossed her head derisively.

'Oh, but don't you want to stay and hear what *I've* learned tonight?'

The strength of anger was flooding through her now. With one kiss he had mastered her again...unmasked her weakness.

'Judging by your expression, I shouldn't think so. But tell me anyway.'

Seeing the tight, hard lines of his face, Claudie's nerve almost failed.

'You don't want to marry me,' she said accusingly. 'You want to marry your legacy.'

His breath hissed inwards and she saw his lithe body stiffen. 'I'm surprised Pascal waited this long.'

'He waited because he wanted to watch the sport. With you as hunter and me as prey.' She felt the acid taste of bitterness on her tongue.

'Is that how you really see it?'

'How else can I see it?' It was almost a plea.

'With your heart and your eyes, not your ears.'

She said coldly, 'What if they tell me the same?'

He trailed his fingers across her cheek to brush gently against her lips. 'They'll see the truth—when you know me a little better.'

'I already know too much.' Claudie jerked away from him, afraid of his power to disturb her with just a touch. 'You're a cold, calculating man with very little conscience,' she ranted. 'If I'd been willing, you would have married me without a word about the stipulations of the will.'

His eyes darkened. 'If you were willing, the will would be merely a side issue.'

'Not to me, it wouldn't.' She stared incredulously into his calm face and her voice rose, laced with a mounting fury. 'How dare you try to use me in that way?'

'I don't agree that I did. But even if it were true, you would hardly be the loser. There would be many compensations.'

'Compensations!' Claudie repeated in tight fury. 'What could possibly compensate for a loveless marriage? For my being lured starry-eyed into the bed of a man with a heart of stone?'

His cheeks creased with a cold smile. 'Not entirely of stone. You're a beautiful young woman. I'm sure a few stars could be arranged.'

'If you were ugly he would still have married you.' Pascal's cruel words rang in her head.

'Oh, thanks!' she jeered, through her pain and dis-illusion. 'I'm sure you're a wonderful actor when the need arises.'

He had moved away, but in two strides he was there again, holding her with one arm and tilting her chin with his free hand, so that she was forced to look into his grim, handsome face.

Her heart lurched with a mixture of fear and un-willing excitement. This close, he seemed all powerful...capable of subduing her most stringent ar-gument with nothing but the strength of his personality.

His cool voice belied the fierce light in his dark eyes.

'When the need for you arises, my sweet Claudie, there's no acting involved.'

The alluring sound of her name on his lips sent strange giddying sensations through her.

His other arm went around her, drawing her close, the sweet warmth of his breath disturbing tendrils of hair on her forehead.

Her face, turned up to his, registered sudden panic and he made a soft tutting sound.

'Don't be afraid of me, *chérie*.' He spoke softly.

'I'm not afraid of you. I just despise you.'

'Perhaps. But you still want me. It is useless you denying it.'

Her voice betrayed her with trembling. 'I don't have to deny anything.'

'I agree. It would be pointless.'

He was right, she acknowledged silently, full of anguish at her own futile weakness. With him this close, his magnetism overpowered even the force of her anger and her treacherous heart beat with a surging excitement as he loomed over her.

But she went on trying. 'And do you deny that you deliberately set out to make me fall in love with you to gain your own ends?'

'No. I don't deny it.'

Claudie's mouth dropped in astonishment. She swallowed hard. 'You mean you admit everything that...has...happened between us...was a fake?'

His dark eyes glowed with threatening intensity. 'Nothing was fake. You know that as well as I.'

He moved closer, his hold imprisoning her against his hard body, forcing her head back. It was impossible to escape. And worse...she knew she didn't want to.

Her lips parted in unwilling invitation as his head dipped, bringing his mouth to hers. He kissed her slowly, exploring the soft contours of her lips. As her own softened in response, he gave a little grunt of satisfaction.

His arms tightened, one hand sliding down to the slim arch of her waist and lower, drawing her more closely against him, where she felt the heat and hardness of him.

He lifted his lips to murmur against her sensitised ear, 'I couldn't fake this, *chérie*.'

His words, and her hand held against him, sent disturbing tingles to every part of her body...quickened her already racing pulse...shortened her breath.

His hand lifted to her breast where her heart beat madly beneath his fingers. 'Nor you this.'

She jerked back fiercely. 'Is this meant to prove something?'

He drew her back against him, his hand moving sensuously against the Judas hardening of her breasts, making her breath catch in her throat.

'Only that things aren't always as they seem.'

He brushed his lips along the soft skin of her throat, searing a path of fire there. She was powerless to stop the shiver of delight that swept through her. In the grip of panic, she tried to wrench herself away, but he held her with cruel strength.

'Let me go,' she said hoarsely.

'Say you don't want me, Claudie, and I will.' He kissed her eyelids, closed in unwilling ecstasy, the corners of her mouth, her throat. 'Or, better still—say you'll marry me.'

She twisted in his grasp. 'Never. Never. Never.'

With a suddenness that had her reeling back, he released her, standing back to stare into her anguished eyes.

'Never is a long time, *chérie*.'

Her breasts rose and fell with each ragged and furious breath.

'Especially for you,' she bit back. 'Time must be running out fast.'

'But not my patience.' To her surprise, he laughed. '*Au revoir* again, *mignonne*. And, once again, sweet dreams.'

CHAPTER SEVEN

CLAUDIE woke just at dawn and found it was impossible to go on lying in bed.

There had been a loud storm during the night, but its crashing reverberations had been nothing compared to the storm of feelings the evening's events had released. The subject of Armand Delacroix and his humiliating proposal had finally exhausted itself, along with her tears, and this morning her mind felt oddly numb. But her body was full of a painful restlessness that, she knew, only physical activity would alleviate.

Looking through the kitchen window as she drank her coffee, she saw, with a kind of ache tugging at her heartstrings, that the landscape was softly lit and drenched by last night's rain, which had now mercifully stopped. It was a scene that simply cried out to be captured in oils, but since she'd arrived she hadn't even attempted to touch her paints.

She realised bitterly that, since the first day, Armand Delacroix had taken up her thoughts, almost to the exclusion of everything else. And today was no different.

After breakfast, she took a walk along the narrow road which skirted around the far side of the main house, leading to the village. Half an hour later, it came into view. It was still early and the place was quiet, the streets deserted, except for one woman at work in her small front garden.

'*Bonjour, madame,*' Claudie offered politely.

'Hello there.' Twinkling, green eyes met hers over the stone wall.

'Well, hello,' Claudie returned, as recognition dawned.

'You've come to pay me a visit, I hope,' Jacqueline Di Maio said.

'I've come for some bread, actually. But I'll stop a while if you really want.'

'I want.' Jacqueline bounded forward to open the gate, reminding Claudie of a friendly, exuberant pup.

'Watch your skirt on the rose bushes. They're getting a bit out of hand.'

Claudie squeezed past and was led across the small lawn to an even smaller patio and offered an ornate iron chair to sit on.

'Have you time for a drink?'

'I would love a small coffee, thanks.' Claudie leaned back and sighed. It was pleasantly warm at this early hour, but a cloudless sky warned that it would soon be hotting up.

As they sat comfortably sipping their drinks, Jacqueline asked, 'How are you enjoying life at St Julien?'

'I love it.'

Jacqueline nodded. 'And the house?'

'I love that too.'

Claudie had a feeling this was leading up to something.

'Look,' Jacqueline began tentatively. 'I'm sorry if I put my foot in it last night. Armand looked real mad at me, as though I'd released a state secret or something, but I thought everybody knew about the will.'

'Everybody probably did,' Claudie said drily. 'Except me. But I do know now.'

'My big mouth again. Still, you were bound to find out sooner or later.'

'It wasn't you. Pascal told me later.'

The French girl sighed with relief. 'Strange, isn't it?'

'Very.' Claudie frowned. 'I still can't believe Annelise would do such a thing. She must have realised it was wrong.'

'Right or wrong, it's certainly caused a stir of excitement around here.' Jacqueline looked thoughtful. 'I wonder if he'll do it. Marry someone, I mean, just for the legacy.'

Claudie's answering smile was grim. 'I'm sure he'll try. He has a lot to lose.'

Jacqueline's next remark was a surprise.

'Not that much. He's very rich in his own right and doesn't really need the money.' She shook her head. 'No. I reckon that if he does do it, it'll be because he can't stand to see the estate go to that headstrong young cousin of his, Pascal Dubret.'

Claudie sighed. 'Does he hate Pascal so much?'

The French girl shrugged. 'I think it's more a question of keeping St Julien in the family. And quite frankly I don't blame him. Pascal has no Delacroix blood. His divorced mother married Annelise's brother when Pascal was twelve or thirteen and he's always been in trouble of one sort or another since then.'

Claudie was silent for some time. What she'd just learned placed the situation in a slightly different light. She had thought Armand desperate to keep the estate for his own gain. Now it seemed to have more to do with keeping Pascal from getting it. But although it changed things, it didn't make his proposal any less despicable. He was still prepared to marry for his own ends. 'Armand said he had a business in Paris. Do you know what it is?'

Jacqueline nodded. 'He has a fashion business.'

Claudie gaped. 'He sells clothes?'

'What else is fashion?' Jacqueline laughed. 'He got involved about ten years ago, when he was sweet on one of the top models. They later went into business together and made a fortune. Delphine Valette. Are you old enough to remember her?'

Claudie laughed. 'Of course. She was one of my favourite models, in fact. I've always liked French haute couture. At college, some of my best designs were inspired by it.'

Jacqueline's brows rose. 'You design clothes?'

'I try. But I'm only at the beginning of my career. I've got a long way to go.'

'You should show them to Armand,' Jacqueline said drily.

'I already have. In fact, after he'd seen one of my dresses, he asked if I could show him some more of my work. He seemed quite taken with the designs I showed him and suggested I make up a portfolio of my best ones.' Claudie coloured. 'I didn't rush, because I wasn't sure he was serious.'

'If he asked, he's serious,' the French girl said. 'Let him have them quick and treat him sweet; it might do you a lot of good, in more ways than one. After all, he has to marry a local girl. And you're the prettiest local girl around.'

Claudie's independent nature was revolted. 'As though I'd let that influence me! I'd get far more satisfaction out of being successful on my own than from being handed a short-cut on a plate by a man with his own selfish reasons in mind.'

'So, even if he asked you to marry him with a promise to boost your career, you'd say no?' The girl's fair brows rose quizzically. 'You'd turn down an irresistible package like that?'

'That's right. In fact he's...' Claudie closed her mouth with a snap. She'd been about to say that he'd already proposed and that she'd turned him down, but

Jacqueline had shown a marked inability to keep a secret and none of this was really anybody's business but her own... and Armand's.

'He's what?' Jacqueline's eyes gleamed with delighted curiosity.

'I was going to say that he's probably forgotten all about it by now.'

Not exactly true, but an acceptable deviation, since she really did believe her dress designs were a side issue to the main one—to persuade her into marrying him.

She added decisively, 'And if he doesn't mention it again, neither shall I.'

When she got back home, Armand was sitting on her balcony in the shade of the vines, with his long legs stretched out against the rail and looking perfectly at ease. He rose to greet her as she ran lightly up the steps.

He seemed to tower over her, his personality overpowering her senses, making them reel. Staring up into his lean, powerful face, Claudie felt the now familiar surge of excitement.

She said ironically, 'Another visit so soon?'

He followed her stiff back into the house where, in the living-room, she turned to confront him.

He put both his hands on her shoulders, demanding her attention. Was it her imagination, or was there a possessiveness about his hold? She pulled back and said sharply, 'If you've come to repeat your proposal, then don't. The answer is still no.'

His grip on her shoulders tightened and he gave her a little shake, making an irritable sound, as though dealing with a fractious child.

'For heaven's sake, girl. You make it sound as though I've insulted you by asking you to marry me. Can't you see what I'm offering you?'

Claudie gave a humourless laugh. 'Very clearly *not* your undying love.'

He grimaced. 'Or the promise of a life full of champagne and roses and happy ever after. I thought you more of an individualist than that. Do you want nothing for yourself beyond the stereotype marriage?'

She snapped back, 'Anything I want, I can get for myself by working for it. *I* don't have to marry to have it handed me on a plate.' She tossed her hair back from her flushed face. 'Which is part of the bargain you're offering, isn't it? The carrot to lead the horse in the direction you want it to go.'

'An interesting remark, but I don't understand.' His calm seemed of the dangerous variety.

Claudie disentangled herself from his hold and went and stood by the fireplace, where she felt a great deal safer, in more ways than one.

'I think you do. The hints of help with my career. They were all part of the inducement, weren't they? Marrying you would be an Open Sesame into the fashion world via your company. But if I'm not interested in your offer then neither are you.'

He went and made himself comfortable on the settee, eyeing her darkly for several moments before bothering to answer.

'On the contrary,' he said, deceptively mild. 'Your dress designs are good enough to sell themselves. Whether I take them or not, they will get there in the end. I'm not foolish enough to let personal issues interfere with good business.'

Claudie made a wry sound. 'So my refusal to marry you makes no difference to your offer to show my designs to your contacts?'

'Precisely,' he agreed, with a nod of his dark, handsome head. 'Before you rushed in with your assumptions, I was about to ask if you had completed your portfolio. My partner, Delphine Valette, is planning a visit to St Julien shortly. I thought you might wish to meet her. It would be a good opportunity to show her some of your designs. She may have some concrete ideas as to their presentation.'

Claudie frowned. 'Then you really are serious?'

'Of course. Would I be wasting my time if I weren't?'

'I don't know.' She lowered her eyes from his penetrating gaze. 'But you'll be wasting your time if you think it will make any difference to the way I feel about marrying you.'

'That's a separate issue, *chérie*,' he said with a smile curving his lips. 'And on that subject I'm quite happy to wait and see.'

She said scathingly, 'If you want to waste even more time on that matter, that's your affair. I won't argue with you.'

He stood up and came towards her, standing close, but not touching her, which was more unnerving than if he had.

'Perhaps that's because you can't.' There was a mocking light in his dark eyes that told her she was in danger of losing this battle. 'Or because you really don't want to.'

He touched her then, his hands gripping her upper arms with tensile strength. 'Perhaps you'd really prefer to agree.'

She bit into her soft underlip and turned her head away, avoiding him as his mouth descended towards hers.

He gave a little laugh and brushed his lips along the soft skin of her throat, searing a path of fire there. She was powerless to stop the shiver of delight that swept through her. In the grip of panic, she tried to wrench herself away.

'Let me go, damn you,' she cried. 'Unless you want me to scream.'

His hold slackened a little and he looked down at her with sardonic amusement.

'Scream away, *ma petite*. It might clear your head and your vision. And afterwards, we will still have a matter to discuss.'

'No. No, we won't.' Claudie's breasts rose and fell rapidly in aggravation. 'Living here might sometimes seem as if we're back in the Middle Ages, but we aren't,' she said tightly, trying to ignore the fascinated attention he was giving her cleavage. 'You can't force me to marry you.'

'Force wouldn't be necessary.' He claimed a lock of her hair and twined strong fingers in the silky tresses...an unnerving gesture of possession. 'We both know that, don't we, *chérie*?'

'Oh!' Claudie ground her teeth in frustration, something she hadn't done since she was a child. She felt as though she was beating her head against a stone wall. Less damage might be done to her feelings if she were! As swiftly as it had returned, her strength was ebbing again.

She said, 'Why don't you ask Miranda? I'm sure she'd jump at the chance.'

She was surprised at the pain she felt even as she said it.

He smiled thinly. 'Perhaps. But then why, *chérie*, should I break your heart?'

Claudie's breath caught angrily in her throat at this clear evidence of his understanding. She searched her whirling brain for words that would finally convince him that she would rather live alone for the rest of her life than take him to fulfil a cold-hearted legacy.

Before she could think, or evade him, he had taken
her hand and carried it to his lips, lingering over the kiss
he placed against her fingers, as erotic as any against
her lips.

Claudie couldn't hide the sharp intake of her breath.

He smiled and released her hand. '*Au revoir*, for now.'

Claudie didn't answer. Neither did she follow him out
into the hall as politeness dictated she should. As she
stood there, slightly dazed but still furious, his head appeared back around the jamb of the door.

'By the way,' he said, 'when you've time, look in the
cellar. I've brought you a bicycle.'

Claudie found the bicycle the following morning. Her
initial reaction was pleasure, followed swiftly by anger.
How dared he try to bribe her with a bicycle? True, it
was a very nice one. A little old-fashioned in style but
with five gears making for easier cycling of the narrow
hilly roads. It even had a finely woven basket attached
for her shopping. It made her want to leap on and take
off immediately, but she was damned if she'd give him
that satisfaction.

She returned to the house to ponder his motives a little
more carefully. It wasn't easy to decide. There had been
moments, in the past weeks, when he had been kindness
itself, and if it weren't for his proposal and the circumstances behind it the gift would have made her very
happy.

As it was, the bicycle intrigued her enough to make
her return later to the cellar and bring it out into the
sunshine. The saddle was well padded and obviously
comfortable, in contrast to the hard, pointed ones
favoured by more dedicated cyclists.

Its paintwork was a deep, rich maroon, with white
highlights to relieve the density of colour.

She longed to try it out and here, away from everything, no one would see her if she did. The temptation
was too much after all. She started off a little shakily,
not having ridden for so long, but as her confidence returned she found herself enjoying the exhilaration of the
cool breeze blowing through her long blonde hair and
caressing her bare arms and legs.

The roads were narrow and stony and she had to concentrate to keep her balance, so she was startled to find
herself almost face to face with a racy dark blue sports
car coming around the next bend.

She veered sharply right and fell off into the ditch just
as the car pulled up short. Shaken and dazed, she sat in
the muddy trench for some seconds before her senses
returned.

'*Mon Dieu*! Claudie . . . I thought it was you. Are you
all right?'

Claudie stared up into Pascal's thin anxious face and
gave a wobbly laugh.

'I think so.'

As she struggled to her feet, he offered her his lean
hand to assist.

'Are you hurt anywhere?'

He made to touch her, but she slapped his hands
hastily away. She moved her limbs experimentally.
Beyond a graze on her elbow and a stinging backside
from its sudden hard contact with the ground, there
didn't seem to be any damage.

'No, I don't think so,' she said, brushing ruefully at
her mudstained dress. 'It's my own fault. I should have
stayed in the garden until I'd got my sea legs back.' She
laughed. 'Or should I have said my cycle legs?'

Pascal took hold of her hand, and slid an arm about
her slender waist.

'Let me help you into the car. You may leave that damned bicycle there in the ditch and I will return it to you later.'

Claudie disentangled herself from him and said a little irritably, 'Oh, please don't fuss. It was only a little tumble. I'm perfectly capable of cycling back to the house.'

'Nonsense,' he argued determinedly. 'I can see you're shaking from here. I insist you ride in the car.'

There was something about the firm grip of his hand against her elbow, as he ushered her towards his car, that warned her of a hidden strength in his slim body. She had a sudden feeling he could be quite ruthless in his own interests.

It must run in the family, she mused grimly, as she allowed herself to be deposited in the low seat of the sporty car, though she couldn't help feeling Armand might have the edge over Pascal in that department.

'You will bring it back to me?' Claudie eyed the bicycle where it lay upturned, wheels still spinning slowly in the air. 'It doesn't belong to me.' She gave a hard little laugh. 'It is an unwanted gift.'

'From an admirer?' He shot her an amused look as he sat alongside, making no attempt to start up the car.

'Not exactly,' she said wryly. 'It was a present from...'

Seeing the odd anticipatory gleam in Pascal's dark eyes, Claudie drew to a halt.

He nodded. 'From your *greatest* admirer, no doubt. From Armand?'

'Yes,' Claudie admitted uncomfortably. 'But I intend to return it.'

'Really? Well done!' A cynical little smile curved Pascal's full lips. 'My cousin has obviously failed to appreciate the fact that you are far too intelligent to be bought by such paltry gifts.'

Through clenched teeth, she said, 'Obviously.'

Pascal said, 'Ah! So, unfortunately for him, he has still to find his bride.'

'Yes. And it certainly won't be me.'

Claudie was amazed to find she felt guilty. Discussing Armand with Pascal felt stupidly like a betrayal of trust. How could she possibly feel like that, when it was he who had betrayed her trust?

Pascal watched her closely, a disturbing gleam in his dark eyes.

'Bravo, *ma belle*!' He turned in the narrow confines of the car's sporty seats and took both her hands in his. 'I have been so concerned. It was unfortunate that business took me away where I was not able to protect you from my cousin's self-interest. You cannot know how happy your certainty makes me.'

Claudie found she was beginning to positively dislike Pascal. There was a malice in him that ran deeper than this one issue. And Armand would do well to take his animosity more seriously than he did.

She said mockingly, 'Are you sure your concern isn't in your own self-interest? After all, it is you who gets the estate if he doesn't.'

Pascal's face was alight with an unholy glee that made Claudie squirm.

'I won't deny I am looking forward to my victory. In a little while everything will be mine.' His eyes glowed into hers.

Despite everything, Claudie couldn't help a sneaking feeling of compassion for Armand. She caught herself up with a snap. For heaven's sake, don't start feeling sorry for the man, she chided herself furiously, hardening her heart. He deserves everything that's coming to him.

To Pascal, she said, sounding strained rather than nonchalant, 'Well, one man's loss...'

'Is another's gain,' he finished jubilantly, and then, with a change of mood, reached out a slim hand to touch against her cheek. 'It could be your gain also, if you were to wish...'

Claudie removed his hand carefully, aware of a frightening undercurrent of fury pushing against her self-control.

'Thank you. But I'm quite happy with my own bequest. And frankly, I'd prefer it if you'd all just leave me to live my own life.'

Pascal's face lit with admiration. 'How refreshing to meet a woman with no ambition to be rich.'

'Not to be rich, perhaps,' she corrected him firmly. 'But I have other ambitions, just as important to me, which some day I hope to achieve.'

'I could, perhaps, help...' he began tentatively

With an angry snort, Claudie cut in. 'Don't even think it. Just take me home.'

CHAPTER EIGHT

CLAUDIE still felt shaky. The fall from the bicycle had left bruises, but the worst hurt had come from Pascal's unthinking confirmation of her suspicions concerning Armand's motives.

She felt bitter and resentful and determined that she would never be taken for a fool by Armand Delacroix. And to think that she had, at one point, actually felt sorry for him!

She couldn't believe her own stupidity. He was the last man in the world she should ever feel sorry for. He had no pity in him for anyone else—certainly not for her anyway. Coming here with his propositions...his compliments...and his bicycles...

She flung herself down furiously into the beautiful old armchair and then winced. Tomorrow she would be sitting upon a bruise to end all bruises if her current soreness in that region was anything to go by. And just look at her elbow and upper arm. It was already beginning to turn red and blue and faintly yellow. She stared at it with resentment and then illogical interest. The mixture of colours was strange, but not unpleasing, she thought and then groaned. It was obviously time to calm down before she really went mad.

She slumped back with a heavy sigh. What was the point of getting herself all worked up like this? After all, none of this was really her problem. It wasn't even as though she was really in love with him. Her feelings were a throwback to a childhood infatuation. In time, she'd get over it. If she could just go on remembering that, it should be simple enough to remain detached.

But, if not actually broken, her heart felt as heavy and as dull as lead. It weighed within her like a pall.

She was suddenly aware of the heat... too hot even for righteous anger. The weather was sultry and sticky and she felt suddenly exhausted.

Transferring herself to the sofa, she stretched out and closed her eyes. No wonder the continentals insisted on their long lunch-breaks. Perhaps it really was only mad dogs and Englishmen who went out in the midday sun. Sensible people took a little siesta. Was that the same word in French? she wondered inconsequentially.

Her rambling thoughts slowed to a trickle as sleep gradually overcame her senses. It was so pleasant just to lie here, in her own deliciously peaceful house...

'Claudie! Claudie! Are you all right?'

Claudie was brought out of her slumber by a rough hand shaking her shoulder and an urgent voice that was annoyingly familiar.

'Wake up, *chérie*! Do you need a doctor?'

Opening her eyes, she stared resentfully up into the anxious face of Armand Delacroix.

'Of course not,' she said crossly. 'Why on earth should I need a doctor?'

He sighed heavily and dropped his hand back on to his knee. He was sitting on the edge of the sofa, leaning over her, and as she struggled to sit up he straightened.

'I saw your bicycle upended in the ditch and came to find out what had happened. When I saw you like that... unconscious... I thought perhaps...'

'I wasn't unconscious,' Claudie argued irritably. 'I was trying to get a little sleep.'

His cheek creased in a grimace of a smile. 'I should have known better than to fear for you.'

Wakened so suddenly, Claudie was still groggy. 'You probably feared I'd sue you,' she said grumpily. 'And if I'd come to any real harm I would have. After all, I didn't ask you to bring that rotten bicycle.'

He laughed shortly. 'That didn't stop you riding it. How was I to know you'd make a mess of it?'

He reached out to brush the tousled hair from her temple and she slapped at his hand irritably, wincing as she jarred her painful elbow.

'Drat!' she exclaimed and lifted it to view its psychedelic bruising once more. 'It still hurts like mad.'

Armand Delacroix saw it too and swore sharply. '*Mon Dieu*! Little idiot!' He took her arm and examined it with unexpected gentleness and Claudie found herself entranced by the thick, dark fringe of his lashes as he looked down. Hastily she looked away, afraid that, with his head so close to her heart, he might hear its sudden hammering.

'You are lucky it isn't broken,' he said, coming out of his absorption. 'Have you injured yourself elsewhere?'

Claudie gave him a rueful grin. 'One other place, but I'm not going to let you see that. Just take my word that I won't die of it.'

'Then I suppose things could have been worse.' He replaced her arm with a shake of his handsome head. 'I thought, when I first saw the cycle in the ditch, that it was there because of that nasty little temper of yours. Now I think you must have fallen into it.'

So he'd noticed that she sometimes flew off the handle! Well, perhaps that was all to the good, since he would realise now that she was going to be no pushover.

'I did,' she admitted, adding testily, 'Would you mind if I put my feet down now?'

He got up and waited for her to rearrange herself on the sofa before sitting down again beside her.

She stole a glance at his profile, which was, as usual, enigmatic.

'It was a split-second choice between the ditch or the wheels of Pascal's sports car.'

Armand's face darkened ominously, as it always did when his cousin was mentioned. 'Pascal! That fool! He always drives too fast. He will kill someone one day.' His nostrils pinched angrily. 'Mercifully, this time, it wasn't you.'

'It wasn't really his fault.' Fair-minded, as always, Claudie rushed to Pascal's defence. 'There was a bend in the road. Impossible for either of us to have seen . . .'

'Beside the point, when in all probability he was driving too fast for the narrow roads.'

Claudie shrugged. 'There seems little point in arguing about it now, since I'm all right.'

'That's a matter of opinion.' His voice was curt. 'I will ask the good doctor to call on you, just to make sure.'

'You'll do no such thing.' Angry colour flooded her cheeks. He still thought he could get away with playing the high-handed host. 'If I need a medical opinion, I'm quite capable of getting one for myself.'

He made a derisive sound. 'You must forgive me if I don't accept your estimate of your capabilities quite so readily now, *chérie*.'

'One unavoidable fall doesn't make me an incompetent,' she shot back hotly. 'And on the question of forgiveness, I forgive you nothing. Now I know the full facts, I can only despise you even more.'

'The full facts? About what?'

'The will, of course. You didn't tell me about the other stipulations.'

'Why should I? They are nobody's concern, except mine.'

'Nobody's concern!' Claudie echoed, aghast. 'It would be very much the concern of any woman who might be foolish enough to agree to marry you.'

'I have only asked one woman,' he said coldly. 'And you haven't accepted.' He shrugged his broad shoulders. 'So?'

'And I never will accept,' Claudie said tartly. 'Especially now I know it would last only a year, during which you have to be forced to remain faithful.'

'Nonsense! That will never be necessary.' His eyes glittered ominously, but Claudie stood her ground.

'Annelise seemed to think it was.'

He gave a short laugh. 'Then Annelise should have known better. When I marry, it will be to a woman to whom it will be no hardship to remain faithful. I would settle for nothing less.'

Claudie stared at him resentfully. Then Pascal had been right. It would take a woman he found at least attractive enough to keep his interest for a year.

Her chest heaved. 'Then it's a pity you didn't explain that to Annelise before she died. Then she wouldn't have gone to her grave worrying you would be a womaniser all your life.'

She was startled by the speed with which his colour drained away. 'Which would be no acceptable concern of hers. Annelise should have known better than to interfere with my life. I will not be ruled from the grave.'

Claudie smiled thinly. 'At least she made it only a year. You should be grateful for that.'

'I am grateful to Annelise for only one thing. And for that, I forgive her all her errors of judgement.'

His gaze caught hers, hard and penetrating, and for a few seconds Claudie wondered anxiously what he was searching for. Whatever it was, there was no way she could hide it from such a probing scrutiny.

It was almost a relief when the stare gave way to a gleam of malicious humour.

'The year could be extended, at my discretion, of course.' He paused meaningfully. 'Depending on the responsiveness of the woman.'

The cruel twist at the corner of his mouth had Claudie's blood boiling.

'And wouldn't that depend on your prowess as a lover?' she retaliated.

He lifted a dark, mocking brow. 'There is no doubting that.'

She said bitingly, 'Experience isn't the only thing that counts in that respect. Some people would prefer a warm, loving heart.'

'I'm sure.' The expression in his eyes changed subtly, flicking over her with a smoky look that had her pulses racing uncomfortably. 'Wouldn't it be wonderful if, as well as all else, one were to find such a heart?'

'So you could have the pleasure of breaking it at the end of a year?'

'What a strange opinion you seem to have of me, chérie.'

He reached out suddenly to cup a hand against her cheek. The electric effect was instant and Claudie pulled back sharply.

'My opinion fits the facts.'

'Does it?' His tone was scornful. 'Ah, yes! We're back to the facts! Pascal's version, naturally.'

Claudie snorted. 'Do you mean there's another?'

'Of course! When you know Pascal a little better, you may cease to swallow every word he says with quite such naïveté.'

'And yet, you would be quite glad for me to swallow yours, without so much as pausing for thought.'

'You don't have to trust to my words, *chérie*. As I've said before, you just have to listen to your heart. It is strange that you cannot learn that lesson. Perhaps it needs to be repeated.'

His laughter was soft, dangerous... but Claudie was too late to heed its warning, as he reached for her.

As his head dipped, she started, but he held her gently, his lips brushing hers, feather-light, setting her heart pounding fiercely. She froze as he kissed her again, his lips barely touching hers, and she closed her eyes. It was agonising, held loosely in his arms this way, a prisoner none the less to his next tantalising onslaught.

'Claudie, look at me,' he commanded, and slowly her eyes came open to meet the piercing gaze that was magically as soft as the darkest sea, shot gently through by a glimmer of moonlight. 'I don't want you to pretend this isn't happening.'

Tenderly, he brushed the heavy hair away from her face, his fingers tucking the strands behind her strangely sensitised ears, sending trickles of delight through her. His lips brushed lightly against her temple, her cheeks, tormentingly against the corner of her mouth, making her turn her head to meet his mouth fleetingly with a kiss of her own.

He gave a grunt of satisfaction and his dark eyes blazed with light, captivating in its intensity.

His arms were hard as he gathered her close, covering her mouth with his in a kiss that scorched and burst into a flame she knew she had been fighting since the beginning. She shouldn't be kissing him back this way, but it was too late now. Her arms wound tightly around his neck, holding him, her prisoner as much as she was his.

A part of her was deeply shocked. Never had she felt such a reaction to a man, never craved satisfaction of the feelings his loving aroused. Feelings she had yet to understand, but which, in this pulsating moment, were undeniable.

He shifted slightly to get closer, his strong arms near to crushing her slender form, his lips reclaiming hers in sweet, hungry passion that brought undreamed-of desires surging through Claudie's unawakened body.

She clung to him, pressing herself against him, hearing the wild thudding of her own heartbeat mingling with the pounding beat of his.

This was madness and yet pure delight. A little cry was torn from Claudie's throat...an urgent plea for...

His arms, which should have been holding her even closer, had begun to slacken and then his mouth was lifted from hers, leaving her hanging on the edge of some aching abyss. Her eyes opened in pained surprise.

'I think we'd better leave it there, *chérie*.'

His own eyes were still bright, his chest still heaving, but his voice was as cool as spring water.

Claudie, still dazed, could only stare at him.

'Did you have any trouble forming an opinion from your own evidence, Claudie?' he asked quietly. 'Real inside information is the only reliable source.'

Feeling as though she had been slapped in the face, Claudie gasped, too choked by an overwhelming mixture of emotions to retaliate at once.

He nodded kindly. 'I can see you're still mulling things over.'

'And when I've finished——' Claudie suddenly found her voice '—my verdict is likely to be unprintable.' She took a deep breath and drew herself up to her full height, which still only brought her head up to his chest. 'I'd like you to leave, Monsieur Delacroix. And, in future, I don't think we shall have too much to talk about, so there would be no point in you coming back here again.'

He shook his head and sighed. 'Oh, I'll be back, Claudie. Now I know how much you want me.'

In the event, Claudie didn't return the bicycle. Mentally, she accepted it as some recompense for her pain and humiliation, which it went some way towards alleviating.

In the days that followed, as she became fitter and her strength increased, she cycled further and further afield.

The area was full of wonderful sights. Towns with houses built high up into the towering rock, some rooms of which were actually transformed caves. Villages that went back to medieval times, with doors of original oak and windows of ancient stained glass. Vineyards with stately *châteaux*, wide gleaming rivers, quiet shaded country roads and farmland vistas. It was all magical and Claudie felt herself falling deeply in love with her new home. When the time came, how would she be able to bear to leave it?

But, thankfully, that wasn't something she had to think of yet and, if it wasn't for the fiasco with Armand Delacroix, she would be blissfully happy.

She wondered if he'd found another 'local' yet. Strangely, it gave her no satisfaction to know he would be forced to make another choice soon or lose his inheritance. Despite his proud boast that he would not be ruled from the grave, he would have to be if he didn't want to lose everything.

Her question was answered one evening when she accompanied Pascal into one of the really exclusive restaurants of the area.

Pascal had telephoned with his invitation and, in a weak moment, she had accepted.

She'd taken pains with her toilette, using subtle make-up shades to suit the aquamarine colour of her eyes and

accentuate the paler hue repeated in her dress. During
one of her delightful foraging expeditions around the
markets she'd come upon the material and known immediately how she would work it up. The result of her
endeavours had been very satisfying indeed, the slim lines
accentuating her gentle curves with a subtle
sophistication.

She wore her hair in a smooth gleaming coil, which
heightened the delicacy of her bone-structure, smooth
chin-line and gracefully curving neck.

At her throat, and in her ears, were pendants of
matching stones in filigree silver, jewellery she cherished
because it had been made by her grandfather and given
to her for her eighteenth birthday, just before he died.

Walking just ahead of Pascal, she saw Armand
Delacroix before he saw her, and faltered a little. He was
sitting at a discreet corner table with, of all people,
Miranda Belling.

He looked remote and incredibly handsome, Claudie
noted, with a strange little ache in the region of her heart.
Miranda looked stunning, in a slightly hard way, and
both seemed engrossed in each other.

Pascal, noting Claudie's hesitation, followed the direction of her gaze and she saw him smile . . . a narrow-
lipped smile without humour.

'Well, well. It looks as though Cousin Armand hasn't
quite given up after all.'

He took Claudie's arm and led her, reluctantly, across
to the table at which Armand and Miranda were seated.

'Good evening.' Pascal was obviously enjoying
himself, an enjoyment that seemed to increase as Armand
looked up with an expression that was far from cordial.

'*Bonsoir*.' He gave Pascal a curt nod and then turned
a hard look upon Claudie, whose colour had already
begun to mount. Why couldn't Pascal have withdrawn

unnoticed? she wondered resentfully; but she knew it would be too much to expect him to pass up an opportunity to disconcert his cousin.

It occurred to her suddenly to wonder whether Pascal had in fact known his cousin would be here and had brought her along to kill two birds with one stone: to annoy Armand and to give Claudie the visual evidence of his cousin's womanising.

'And good evening to you, Mademoiselle Drew.' Armand's hard gaze swept her coolly from head to toe with a flickering glance that showed no hint of approval.

She did not miss the significance of his formality. He was obviously angry. 'I have called upon you a number of times, but you have not been at home.'

She answered defiantly, 'No. I have been out and about.'

'As, it appears, you have yourself, cousin,' Pascal cut in. He lifted Miranda's hand to his lips. 'You look very lovely tonight, Miss Belling.'

Miranda gave him a pleased smile. 'Thank you.'

Claudie silently acknowledged the truth of Pascal's comment. Miranda certainly was a very attractive girl, if you liked the hard, confident type, and Armand obviously did.

His gaze was on Claudie once more. 'I presume there is no need to ask if you are enjoying life.'

Before she could answer, Pascal cut in.

'You presume correctly. In fact, we have both had a most enjoyable few days playing at tourist. I can't understand why I haven't done so before.' He placed a proprietorial arm about Claudie's shoulders. 'But then, I've never been lucky enough to have such an enchanting companion to spur me.'

Embarrassed by the lie and by his familiar gesture, Claudie tried surreptitiously to dislodge his hold, but he only grasped her more firmly.

'I'm sure it's Miss Drew who feels she's the lucky one.'

Miranda Belling spoke up suddenly. Her eyes swept insultingly over Claudie.

'Is this another of your delightfully home-made concoctions, Miss Drew? I must say you're to be congratulated on a good effort.'

'It's hand-made, yes,' Claudie said tightly, shooting a furious glance at Armand Delacroix, who, it was obvious, had been discussing her business with his secretary. 'As Monsieur Delacroix may also have told you, I design purely for myself.'

'A wise decision, I'm sure.' The girl's wide mouth stretched in a polite smile. 'The dress is very pretty, but if I may say so——'

'I think you may already have said too much,' Armand's hard voice cut in, and the look he gave her withered her visibly.

To Claudie, he said, 'My apologies.'

'You don't have to apologise,' Claudie said woodenly, wishing it was possible simply to disappear from the spot by magic. 'I'm sure it's not that important.'

'You're wrong. The matter is very important, particularly to you, and I propose to call on you tomorrow to discuss it.'

'Then you had better make your call an early one,' Pascal cut in smilingly. 'Claudie and I have a rather full day planned for tomorrow. Haven't we, *ma belle*?'

As she looked from one pair of hard eyes to the other, Claudie's temper suddenly snapped.

'No, Pascal! We haven't! I am not your *belle* and I refuse to become a bone between two unpleasant dogs,' she cried furiously. 'Tomorrow, I shall be at home to neither of you.'

Turning on her heel, she left the restaurant, unconcerned, for the present, at the curious stares that followed her hasty progress. Outside, in the cool of the evening, she took deep steadying breaths, determined to keep the threatening tears at bay. What was she crying about anyway? Certainly not Miranda's characteristic bitchiness, nor the childish performance of two grown men?

But she knew it was more than that, however reluctant she might be to acknowledge it. Somehow, it seemed to make things so much worse to know that it was Miranda Belling who had been his second choice.

'*Chérie*! I am so sorry.' Pascal had followed her quickly.

For one wild moment she had been tempted to leave for home alone, but it was a futile impulse. There was no way she could have done so.

'Pascal, you are a hypocrite,' she rounded on him. 'You are not at all sorry. In fact, you're all too obviously very happy. It's quite obvious you planned this to get back at Armand.'

As he made to interrupt, she waved a furious hand at him. 'But that's between you and him. I just won't stand, any longer, for the way you keep trying to drag me into it.'

Despite her efforts to evade him, he caught both her hands in his, holding her so that she was turned towards him. His eyes gleamed maliciously and Claudie realised she was beginning to dislike Pascal very much.

'But, my sweet Claudie, you were already in it. Even before you arrived here, it was so.' He laughed softly. 'Annelise put you on the spot. A ripe little plum, just ready to drop into the greedy hands of her darling Armand.'

Claudie wanted to put her hands over her ears, to block out the venom.

'Stop saying that,' she managed to croak past the huge lump that had risen in her throat. 'Annelise left me my house and that's all that concerns me.'

'Come, Claudie!' he said, with an ironic little smile, and she was suddenly aware of the hard glimmer of hatred behind the brown eyes. 'You are not so naïve that you cannot see what is plain. You are her last sacrifice to him. She knew he would use you . . .'

'Oh! You . . .' Lost for words to express the revulsion that was twisting in her stomach, she wrenched her hands free, and struck out at him blindly, making contact only by instinct with his thin cheek.

'And what of you?' Her fury was almost out of control. 'Do you think I don't realise that you are playing the same horrible twisted game? Well, I want no part of it. Do you hear?' She was shouting, her voice ringing clearly in the night.

Suddenly, Pascal was thrust aside and it was Armand Delacroix's dark face that confronted her now.

'Get a hold on yourself,' he ordered curtly. 'Pascal is not the only one to hear.'

Her blazing temper was turned on him, the real cause of all her ills.

'Why should I care?'

'An understandable attitude,' he said, with a strained smile. 'But unwise, if you intend to go on living here.'

Claudie was no longer sure she wanted to go on living here. If there was even the smallest glimmer of truth in what Pascal had just said about Annelise using her as bait for Armand . . .

He took her arm. 'Get into my car. I'll drive you home.'

'Claudie is my guest...' Pascal began belligerently, but stopped, transfixed by his cousin's ferocious glare.

'You had better go,' he commanded, 'before I give you what you deserve, and our interested onlookers a sight they'll find it hard to forget.'

'Brave words.' Pascal ground the words between his teeth. 'The time will come when I shall see if the deeds they promise are as brave.'

'I await that day with pleasure,' Armand assured him fiercely. 'Meanwhile, you may escort Miranda Belling back to the house.'

Miranda had now appeared, her expression a mixture of apprehension and stubborn defiance.

To her, he said, in a clipped voice, 'You will be in my office at eight o'clock sharp tomorrow morning.'

He didn't wait for her response, nor for a final glance at Pascal's glowering face. He took Claudie's arm and led her towards his gleaming silver car.

She got in without a word, too confused and miserable to refuse.

Throughout the journey back to her house, he spoke not a word. His expression was thunderous and he seemed to be containing his fury only by an extreme effort. Even in this black mood, Claudie had to admit he looked superb, every bit the cold French aristocrat. But, beneath that cold façade, Claudie had been given a glimpse of a heated passion, which, if it were teamed with true love...

She caught herself up with a little gasp. For heaven's sake...she hated the man. He had had the gall to think he had merely to snap his fingers and she would come running, and she had shown him different.

Let him try his wiles now on the hapless Miranda Belling. She was more than welcome to him and all the pain that would bring.

But it was her own pain that she had to contend with now.

They had reached her front door before he said firmly, 'Don't bother to argue. I'm coming inside.'

She said grittily, 'Be my guest.'

In the living-room, she faced him. 'Did you wish to speak to me about something in particular?'

'Of course, or I wouldn't be here. Sit down.'

She sat and folded her shaking hands in her lap. The evening had been an unnerving one. 'If you are going to propose again, please don't...or I won't be responsible...'

He waved a hand in dismissal. 'You have already made your opinions on that matter perfectly clear.'

Claudie couldn't help a little jolt of surprise. So he really had given up and turned his attentions elsewhere. The warm night seemed suddenly to have turned chilly and she hid a little shiver.

He sat down opposite her and leaned towards her.

'For once, you will listen to what I have to say and take heed.'

Claudie glared at him silently and he went on.

'There is something you must understand about my cousin.'

She blinked in surprise. She had expected something more than petty jealousy. Her mouth opened for a sarcastic retort, but he put up his hand.

'Don't interrupt,' he ordered curtly. 'I don't blame you for your error of judgement. Pascal is a type your kind of girl might not meet with often and he has the ability to blind the unwary with his charm.'

Claudie said ironically, 'If he were a Delacroix, I'd say it ran in the family.'

He took her hand suddenly and held it despite her attempt to pull away. 'Listen to me, Claudie. It's important. Pascal was badly spoilt by his mother. As a consequence he is convinced he has a right to anything he wants. And he can be dangerous if he's thwarted.'

She laughed shortly. 'Something else that runs in the family.'

He released her hand and sighed, leaning back with a resigned expression.

'You are obviously not in the mood to be reasonable. I should, perhaps, leave it for a better time.'

Claudie said bitterly, 'You would still be wasting your time. In future I want nothing to do with Pascal, or with you.'

Her heart pounded. The hurt had started to rise again, along with a vision of her own trusting young face turned to her godmother to speak her dream. Oh, but he would be faithful to me. Had she herself sown the seed?

'Is it true Annelise brought me here deliberately, hoping you would choose to marry me to keep your inheritance?'

She hadn't meant to bring this up with him again, but she didn't seem able to help herself.

'Probably.' He nodded. 'Annelise could sometimes be very wise.'

She stared at him. 'Do you mean you approve?'

'Of her methods ... no.' There was no mistaking now the light that shone in the dark depths of his gaze. 'Of her taste ... entirely.'

Claudie stared in amazement and sank down on to the settee. 'But surely you can't condone what she did?'

He took her hands and came and sat beside her. 'Looking at it from her point of view, who else would she wish to entrust with my happiness?'

'And what about *my* happiness?' she demanded indignantly. 'It was a thoughtless, cruel thing to do. She had no right to trust to luck that things would work out well. Besides, if she'd known me at all well, she would know I could never be happy with a man I didn't love and who didn't love me.'

His hand came beneath her chin, lifting her face up to his. His dark eyes probed hers.

'Don't worry, *chérie*. Even if she didn't know it...I do.'

After he'd gone, she went to bed and lay for long hours, staring dry-eyed at the ceiling.

So! He'd finally given up. And now it was Miranda's turn.

She told herself she was sorry for the girl, but as she lay, staring into the future ahead, she knew she envied her—even with the heartache that was sure to come at the end of the year.

CHAPTER NINE

PASCAL telephoned just after nine o'clock to apologise, but Claudie put the telephone down. She did the same when Armand rang, and after two days the phone stopped ringing.

Claudie should have felt happy to be rid of them both, but instead she felt keyed up and restless, unable to get down to any useful work.

It occurred to her that Armand might be ringing about Delphine Valette's visit, but she reasoned that if that was the case he would find some other way to let her know. And, as the proposed weekend came and went without him making contact, she assumed it had all been part of his strategy to win her over.

The good weather showed no sign of breaking and she rose to yet another azure-blue and cloudless day, which seemed somehow to have lost its magic. She took her breakfast out on to the terrace, wondering where and why it had disappeared.

The sun was already very hot and showed every sign of getting hotter and the thought of a dip in a deliciously cool pool was very enticing, but she pushed the thought away. There was no way she wanted to meet up with the male inhabitants of St Julien. She would make a determined effort to work instead.

But, after working for two hours, getting more uncomfortable by the minute, she gave up the struggle and went to find her bathing suit. With a bit of luck, Pascal would be back in Paris and Armand would be busy, as he usually was at this time of day, with estate business.

But fate, as usual lately, was not on her side. She was dismayed to find Armand swimming slowly up and down the length of the pool, his expression dark and brooding.

His face changed when he saw her, seeming to light up momentarily, before resuming his dark expression.

'This is a pleasant surprise, *chérie*. I didn't know you used the pool.'

'I haven't until now.' Claudie grimaced, wishing she'd had the sense to stay away. 'But it is so hot today, I couldn't resist it.'

He came out and sat on the edge as she took off her robe, his eyes intent on her as she emerged in her bikini.

'I am disappointed. I hoped it was the thought of being with me that you found irresistible.'

She said ironically, 'That too, of course.'

Claudie dropped her robe on a lounger and crossed to him reluctantly for his kiss of greeting and he stood up, taking both her hands in his, holding on as his lips brushed her cheeks.

'You have a superb figure,' he said admiringly, pushing her away a little to get a better view.

'Thanks.' There was something in the hot intensity of his gaze that had her wishing she'd worn her one-piece bathing suit. Carefully, she disentangled her hands from his.

Moving away from him, she dived in cleanly, swimming close to the bottom of the pool, coming up as she touched the wall at the other end.

'Bravo!' he applauded. 'Athletic as well as beautiful.' Jumping into the water, he swam towards her.

'As I think I may have mentioned, *chérie*, we would make a delightful couple, you and I.'

He was beside her now, his tanned face close to hers, his dark hair slicked back, outlining the well-shaped head.

She said tightly, 'Except that we are not a couple.'

His arm slid about her waist. 'We could be.'

She felt the tenuous strength of his fingers as they tightened against her wet skin and was too slow to avoid his lips as they descended on hers.

She let him kiss her, struggling to make no response. Pinned against the slippery tiles and treading water, there wasn't much else she could do. But as the force of his mouth on hers intensified and his body began pressing urgently against hers, she found her resolve beginning to melt and pushed against him strongly, in an effort to disentangle herself.

He drew away a little and laughed. 'You do not like to make love in the water?'

'I have no wish to make love with you in the water or anywhere else,' she said darkly. 'Will you please let go of me?'

He grinned. 'You English women like to think you are liberated. But you do not know how to surrender yourselves to love. Let me show you.'

'You may know a lot about women, English or otherwise, but you know absolutely nothing about me.'

'I know enough to find you fascinating.'

He dipped his head to kiss her again, but she avoided his lips.

'Will you stop this?' She sounded breathless and hated herself for this evidence of his effect on her.

She pushed harder against him and succeeded in getting free. Indignantly, she hauled herself out of the pool, sitting on the edge to recover her breath. But it caught in her throat as he swam towards her.

'Why do you persist in running away from the inevitable?'

'Nothing is inevitable,' she bit back, and would have jumped up, but his hand clasped about her ankle, holding her still.

'You have delightful ankles,' he said musingly. His cool fingers caressed the delicate bones, slid up the calf of her leg, touched against her thigh, making her squirm with all kinds of oddly exciting sensations.

Despite everything, he still had the power to disturb her.

'Don't do that,' she said breathlessly, trying to extricate herself from his hold.

'Why not? I like to touch you.' His expression was suddenly serious, his dark, intent eyes searching hers. 'Why won't you admit that you like it too?'

Claudie stared back helplessly at him, knowing suddenly that he would never give up. Even if she never agreed to marry him, he would wield his power over her in cruel punishment.

'Why should I lie to please you?' Pride rose to overcome her weakness and she wrenched free, standing up on legs that felt like jelly, walking rather shakily to where she'd left her robe.

But before she had time to put it on he was there beside her, spinning her around by the arms to face him.

'Claudie! Wait! I have something I wish to tell you.'

'Maybe you do,' she bit back furiously. 'But I have no wish to listen to it.'

'But you will listen anyway.'

She opened her mouth for an angry retort, but, as her lips parted, his mouth descended again to hers, its sweetness, as always, undermining her strength. Her body yearned to mould itself against him. She fought the urge, but she was fighting a losing battle, and he knew it, as her bones began to melt. The deepening of his kiss, the small triumphant sound deep in his throat, released her from the spell.

Angrily she wrenched back. 'The ultimate weapon,' she cried harshly. 'But one in plentiful supply. Do you think you are the only man who has aroused me?'

His face paled a little. 'I do not need to be told what passion lies beyond those wide, innocent-seeming eyes. It is there in your smile... in the provocation of your every movement.' He smiled thinly. 'But you lie. The deep fires of love have yet to be kindled in you. And I will award myself that pleasure.'

'That pleasure isn't yours to award!' Claudie said, with a dignity it was hard to maintain when half naked in her despised bikini. Humiliation mixed with her fury. What right did he think he had to be saying such things to her?

His arms closed tightly about her and his mouth aimed purposefully at hers. Twisting her head forcefully away, she avoided him and he growled in angry frustration.

'What am I doing, *chérie*, that is so wrong?' His voice had become low and seductive. 'You are a beautiful woman and I want to hold you, to kiss you.'

Cold as ice, she said, 'That's your problem.'

Abruptly, he released her. 'So it would seem,' he said slowly, and took her robe from her, holding it for her to slip her arms into the sleeves.

How could all that fire and passion have been doused so quickly? Claudie wondered dazedly, as she covered her shivering body with the robe, tying the belt tightly at her waist.

He held her arm with detached politeness as she slid her feet into her sandals and then slipped his own clothes over his trunks.

He wore shorts and a short-sleeved shirt, impatiently left unbuttoned to reveal the tautly muscular chest and powerful shoulders. Sweat glistened faintly on his forehead and the base of his throat.

There was nothing of the seductive charm about him now. With his hands clenched at his sides and the muscles of his jaw set hard, he looked alert and dangerous.

Claudie shivered.

'Since you've finished here, perhaps you'd be good enough to come up to the house with me. I would appreciate a little private conversation.'

She stared up at him in consternation, seeing no warmth in the piercing eyes. She really didn't think she could take much more today and particularly not from Armand Delacroix. All she wanted to do now was rush home and close the door on everyone.

'Actually, I'm working on my portfolio,' she began and then remembered there was no further need for that particular piece of fiction. She went on, coldly sarcastic, 'Although I take it I missed Mademoiselle Valette's visit...'

He nodded irritably. 'It is that which I wish to speak about.'

She sighed. 'Is there any point in going on with this?'

'That's for you to decide.' As she still hesitated, he gave a short laugh. 'There will be no discomfort involved, I assure you, and I'll try not to keep you too long.'

'Very well,' Claudie gave in grudgingly and let him take her arm. 'If you insist.'

He said nothing as they walked towards the house, seeming intent on his inner thoughts. Which weren't very pleasant, judging by the grim expression on his face.

On arriving at the house, he ushered Claudie into the library off the hallway and disappeared upstairs.

She waited impatiently, feeling at a disadvantage in bikini and robe. With their current associations, it was unlikely she'd ever wear either of the damned things again, she told herself grimly.

He came back in about five minutes, dressed in trousers and casual shirt, and seated himself behind his imposing oak desk. With a brief nod of his head he indicated she should sit in the tall leather chair placed opposite.

There was a heavy frown between his brows and it was obvious he was still very angry. Looking at him a little apprehensively, Claudie wondered how he managed to look even more handsome when he was at his most grim.

Without preamble, he said, 'Delphine Valette sends her regrets that she was unable to meet you here at St Julien. The cancellation of her visit was unavoidable.'

She wondered dismally why he was still bothering to pretend. Did he think he could recover her trust by fabricating this flimsy excuse?

Claudie gave a shrug of pretended unconcern. There was no way she would let him see her disappointment. Because, at the back of her mind, she had obviously been hoping the offer might be genuine and that something might possibly come of it.

'Oh, well! It was good of her to show an interest, but maybe it's just as well, since I don't really think I have anything worthwhile to show her yet. Perhaps in six months or so...'

She tailed off at the impatient shake of his dark head.

'Opportunities are rare phenomena,' he said drily. 'They shouldn't be left to hang fire for six months.'

Claudie felt belligerent. What was he trying to do? Build her up again for another slap-down? But her pride forced her to go on with his game.

'It's hardly my fault if I'm unprepared, when you spring something like this on me out of the blue.'

To her surprise, he nodded in agreement. 'Fair comment. But I am of the opinion that you are wrong about your current designs. And the opportunity hasn't been lost. Delphine has attempted to make it up to you for your disappointment by arranging two seats for the fashion show which keeps her in Paris, and which is to be staged the day after tomorrow.'

Claudie stared at him in real astonishment.

'Well, that's kind, but I really don't think...' she floundered, overwhelmed by the unexpectedness of the offer. 'I mean...I don't have transport, or anyone to go with.'

He gave her a dispassionate look. 'I shall be very happy to take you.'

Claudie's heart skipped a beat as she looked into the cool dark eyes which seemed deliberately unreadable.

'Do you mean you want me to go with you to Paris?' she asked warily.

Seeing her expression, he gave one of his short, un-amused laughs. 'This is an invitation, not an immoral suggestion.'

Perhaps it was also a convenient cover, Claudie thought wildly, remembering Jacqueline's comment that he had once been 'sweet' on the model. Perhaps this was a question of if the mountain couldn't or wouldn't come to Mohammed, Mohammed would go to the mountain...but not too obviously!

She said coolly, 'Thanks for the reassurance and I'll certainly think about it.'

He sighed impatiently. 'The show is in Paris. If you want to go, then we should leave early tomorrow morning. It is many hours' drive to Paris and we would want to arrive in time for an evening meal at the hotel.'

'Do you mean we'd be staying overnight?' Her heart began to thud unevenly.

His sensuous mouth curved mockingly. 'You didn't imagine it could all be done in one day, did you?'

She bit her lip. She still had trouble remembering how big a country France really was. 'No. Of course not. I suppose I just wasn't thinking.'

'The heat, perhaps,' he suggested, sounding ironic. 'Never mind. My car has air-conditioning, and Paris, in the evening, will be cooler.'

Claudie frowned. She was tempted. She had never been to a real fashion show by one of the top couturiers. Any one of her art college friends would have been thrilled to be invited. It was bound to be a glamorous affair...with all the best models...something she would regret missing. The drawback was that she would be going with Armand Delacroix. But, perhaps, she found herself reasoning, with his attentions engaged elsewhere, she might be free to enjoy the occasion.

'Well. Since that's settled——' he stood up decisively, obviously taking silence for agreement '—I'll drive you home.'

Claudie frowned. 'I haven't said I would come.'

'You would be very silly not to.' He came around the desk to take her elbow. 'Don't waste time, Claudie! Accept the challenge.'

She wondered cynically which challenge he was referring to. A weekend spent in his company would certainly be the most daunting.

As they left the library, they passed Miranda Belling, who was on her way in.

Miranda frowned. 'Are you leaving?'

'Yes. I'll be out for the rest of the day and in Paris over the weekend.'

Her mouth compressed a little. 'But I've brought the mail for signing.' She had a file of papers in her hands.

He shook his head. 'None of them is that important. Put them on my desk and I'll sign them when I get back.'

'Very well.' She managed a demure smile, though her eyes were fixed coolly on Claudie's face.

He hesitated and looked suddenly thoughtful.

'On second thoughts, there are one or two which might be better sent off now.' He took the file from her hand and returned to his desk, leaving the two women standing in the doorway.

Miranda's smile had disappeared.

'I'm sure you'll enjoy the show, Miss Drew,' she said, her voice pitched very low. 'They're really terribly well done. And you'll find the hotel most discreet.'

Claudie grimaced, remembering the girl's boast that she and Armand frequently visited the bright lights of Paris together.

'I'm sure I will.'

Armand was back, his eyes flicking from Miranda to Claudie's colour-tinged cheeks. He shook Miranda's hand formally. '*Au revoir.*' To Claudie, he said, 'Let's go.'

She wanted to argue, to demand an explanation of Miranda's barbed remark, which seemed to imply that he would expect Claudie to sleep with him, but thought better of it. Common sense told her it was probably spite. And who could blame the girl, when she was probably hoping against hope to be Armand's final choice of a 'local' girl?

As they walked around the back of the house in the direction of the garage, a man came towards them.

'Hello, there, folks.'

He was a big man with a thatch of white hair, a ruddy complexion and an American accent.

'Can you help? I'm looking for Pascal Dubret.' He pronounced it Doobret.

Armand frowned. 'In what connection?'

The man touched the side of his nose in a conspiratorial gesture. 'A little honest business.'

A wry little smile pulled at the corner of Armand's mouth. 'With Pascal?'

The man seemed to miss the irony.

'Sure. I was waiting at the barn at midday, like he said, but he wasn't there.'

Armand's mouth thinned. 'He was probably delayed. I'm sure he'll be sorry to have missed you. I'll ask him to get in touch.'

'Gee, thanks.'

Armand shook the hand the man held out. 'You're welcome.'

As the man began to walk away, Armand called to him and went across to speak. Claudie saw the American delving into his inside pocket for a card, which he handed to Armand.

His expression was pensive as he returned to Claudie.

At the house, he dropped her off quickly, with an admonition to make sure she was ready by eight-thirty at the latest the following morning.

Claudie wondered if she should thank him for the proposed outing, but after all it was he who was insisting that she go, and she wasn't really quite sure what it was all in aid of.

He kissed her, French-style, on both cheeks, and his hands remained on her shoulders as he looked down at her.

Claudie bit her lip as she found her pulse was already racing. Just the smallest contact with him seemed to set the butterflies fluttering madly inside her.

'You won't be wandering away from the house any more today?'

It seemed more of a command than a question, and Claudie looked up at him in surprise.

'Perhaps. I haven't really thought about it.'

He made an impatient sound. 'You'll have enough to do preparing your luggage. As well as the drawings, I'd like you to bring some of those designs you've made up. Then you'd be wise to retire early.'

'I think I'll survive having to pack a bag,' she said sarcastically. 'I don't yet find a little effort that exhausting.'

'Nevertheless, we're in for a long drive tomorrow and the weekend might get a little hectic.'

'I can hardly wait.'

He laughed and, surprisingly, gave her shoulders a little squeeze before dropping his hands.

'Soon you will find out if the waiting has been worthwhile.'

There was a glint in his dark eyes that seemed strangely like a promise.

Claudie looked hastily away. If she started letting her imagination run riot at this point, she'd be a nervous wreck before they'd even arrived.

Despite everything, she couldn't help feeling excited. Paris, and a fashion show, in the company of Armand Delacroix. No wonder that night she was tossing and turning for long hours before she finally fell asleep.

Armand had been right. The journey to Paris was a long one and Claudie gave a grateful sigh as the car finally pulled into the car park of a large imposing hotel in the centre of town.

She'd worn a lightweight pale lemon suit over a sleeveless cotton shirt and, as she got out of the car, she bent to brush the creases from her skirt.

Straightening up, she found Armand Delacroix's eyes fixed on her, dark and inscrutable. She looked back at him, wondering what was in his mind now, knowing there was little chance she'd ever find out. He really was the most enigmatic man she had ever encountered.

She took a deep breath and looked around at the opulent marble and glass frontage and the small but luxuriant garden that screened it from the street. It was hard to believe that she was actually here in Paris with him ... about to spend the night ...

He'd taken his jacket off in the car, and his shirt was open at the throat, revealing the strong, tanned neck that she found strangely erotic. The sight of it was doing peculiar things to her insides and she looked hastily away.

The touch of his hand against her elbow as he led her up to the hotel entrance seemed possessive and a little *frisson* of excitement shot up her spine.

Curious eyes turned in their direction as they entered and there were respectful greetings from the staff. He was obviously well known here and Claudie couldn't help wondering if there wasn't something in what Miranda Belling had implied.

But if she'd half feared an attempt at seduction, she had little trouble convincing herself it was foolish. He was, after all, in Paris to visit a woman who was more than likely still one of his lovers.

On the journey up, he'd certainly seemed abstracted, making only desultory conversation and keeping well away from personal matters, which suited Claudie. However unlikely, perhaps he had at last taken the hint.

Standing alongside Armand in Reception, Claudie tried hard to make sense of his rapid French, without success. She told herself there was no point in worrying. Armand would hardly be likely to book them in as Monsieur and Madame Smith, without at least trying to

ascertain if she would be willing! Even he wouldn't dare
risk a scene in the hotel lobby if she wasn't.

Nevertheless, she gave a sigh of relief as the recep-
tionist handed him two keys.

With an understanding little smile, he handed her one.
'Adjoining. But not inter-connecting.'

She still seemed to be annoyingly transparent to him.

Now they'd arrived, he seemed more relaxed, and there
was that possessive gripping of her elbow again as he
led her towards the staircase.

They'd reached the second floor and he was coming
to a halt in front of one of the bedroom doors.

'This one is yours, I think.'

He took her key from her hand and opened the door,
stepping back politely to let her enter, making no attempt to go in with her.

Claudie bit her lip, determined not to let him annoy
her.

'I shall be next door.' A wave of his lean hand indicated the next room. 'Dinner is booked for an hour's
time. Meanwhile, call me if you need anything.'

With a formal little handshake, he left her there.

What else could she possibly need? Claudie asked
herself as she looked around the room. Sumptuous, in
a very French way, it had everything...even a
comfortably upholstered and cushioned *chaise-longue*
close to the tall windows.

She was tempted to try it out immediately, but knew
it would be disastrous. She was tired enough to sleep
and there wasn't time for that.

She turned the shower to cool, sighing with appreciation as the silky water ran over her body, reviving
her vitality.

Half an hour later, she was brushing her pale blonde
hair to a lustrous sheen, pinning it back with ceramic

flowers the same shade as the primrose silk blouse she'd now teamed with the skirt of her suit. In her ears were clusters of tiny pearls, which were repeated, interspersed in the fine gold chain about her throat. The pale strappy leather sandals with their spiky heels drew attention to her slim shapely legs and added height and a feeling of glamour.

Claudie studied her reflection in the mirror with a critical eye, deciding the result of her labours had been worth the effort. She wondered whether Armand Delacroix would even notice, since he'd now excluded her from his marriageable list. Well, the less attention he paid to her, the more comfortable she would feel, she thought, as she finished off her toilette with a little light make-up.

A soft coral lipstick, a little tawny eyeshadow and a coat or two of dark brown mascara were all that was necessary to complement the honey gold tan of her skin.

As she'd suspected, he paid no obvious attention to her appearance when he called for her later, his eyes flicking over her almost impersonally as he made a curt little bow over her hand.

Contrarily, she felt peeved. All that effort! And for what?

As he ushered her into the restaurant, heads turned, more female than male ones, Claudie noted drily.

In contrast to his lack of interest, her heart had made an immediate response to the fact that he too had taken obvious pains with his appearance. He looked fantastic in a lightweight navy blue suit with a pearly grey shirt and matching grey and navy tie.

The female eyes, after feasting upon him, turned on Claudie with looks of envy. And who could blame them? She was dining with the most dynamically attractive man in the room. They weren't to know that she was here with him purely on a matter of business. Or was it camouflage for his affair with Delphine Valette?

The meal was delicious and, as usual, he gave it his full attention. They started off with lightly grilled goat's cheese on crisp lettuce with thin slices of tomato and creamed and seasoned avocado.

Claudie murmured her appreciation and he looked up with a little smile of gratification.

'*C'est bon. Oui?*'

'*Oui. Très bon.*'

With her approval, he selected fresh trout, garnished with lemon and parsley and served with fluffy rice and lightly cooked and seasoned red peppers, which tasted wonderful.

She managed the soft white cheese in cassis, the rich redcurrant liqueur of Dijon, but had to forgo dessert from the variety offered on the laden trolley.

His dark brows rose quizzically. 'No room for the finale?'

Claudie shook her head. 'I think I'll stop before I burst.'

He said, with the first hint of humour, 'And what a disaster that would be.'

His dark eyes gleamed at her in a way that had her pulses leaping uncomfortably and if he'd gone on looking into her eyes for much longer he would undoubtedly have seen her excitement. She was glad that, just then, the waiter came to clear away for coffee.

Armand ordered it served out on the terrace. 'The rear garden overlooks an ornamental fountain, which I find most relaxing,' he explained. 'Just looking at water makes one feel cooler, don't you think?'

Claudie had to admit that it did, but she was suddenly reluctant to be outside with him in the seclusion of semi-darkness.

He hadn't mentioned that there was, alongside the fountain, a small dance-floor, or that close by a group of musicians were playing soft music. Coloured lights were strung out among the trees and cast reflections upon the cascading waters, creating a magical atmosphere.

The intimate mood of the place seemed only to accentuate the unromantic nature of their visit.

More and more, she began to feel that this hotel might hold many clandestine associations for him, which were far away from his present situation. Was that why he was so remote from her?

But, after all, from her own choice, she was not his lover. She found herself suddenly wishing that his proposal of marriage had been based on something more than practical considerations.

She stole a glance at him, her heart thudding at the mysterious lines of his handsome face in the dim lighting. He seemed restless, his dark eyes moving about as though he was searching for something, or someone.

And he hadn't long to wait. Delphine Valette created a stir that Claudie felt, even before the model arrived at their table. Heads were turning everywhere, but the model blithely ignored the stares, addressing herself to Armand with a wide, attractive smile.

'Armand, *mon cher*. I thought I would find you here on the terrace. So sorry I couldn't make it for dinner.'

'Well, you're here now. Looking ravishing as always.'

Armand couldn't disguise his pleasure as he stood up, kissing both her cheeks, and then her lips.

He introduced her to Claudie. 'Madame Delphine Valette, Mademoiselle Claudie Drew.'

Madame Valette! Claudie's mind echoed. Delphine was married. So Armand wasn't even above having an affair with a married woman. Given his natural distaste for marriage, it was probably even preferable.

She saw suddenly the irony of what Annelise had done. The one thing in the world Armand wanted now was the thing which previously he had most assiduously avoided . . . marriage.

Delphine kissed her in a cloud of expensive perfume and seated herself at the table.

'Get me a drink, Armand darling, would you? I can't wait for a waiter, I'm positively dehydrated.' She fanned herself with an elegant manicured hand. 'Rehearsals are always much more exhausting than the real thing.'

Claudie watched in amazement as Armand went off to the bar. Here, obviously, was one woman who could command his devotion.

'So. You are the girl who has fired dear Armand's imagination with your talents.'

Delphine's eyes were on her face in open appraisal.

Claudie flushed. 'Monsieur Delacroix has certainly expressed interest in some of my designs.'

'He has a head for business.' The arched brows rose. 'And for unusual beauty. If I know Armand, he is very much interested in the designer also?'

Claudie frowned. Was the model asking Claudie point-blank if she and Armand Delacroix were lovers?

She said stiffly, 'Any arrangement reached will be purely a matter of business.'

Delphine gave a low laugh. 'Is it for you to decide the nature of any arrangement?'

The hazel eyes held an odd gleam that brought a rush of colour to Claudie's cheeks.

Armand had returned with a tray of drinks. He cast the model a disapproving look.

'Come, Delphine! I hope you have not been trying to disconcert Claudie. You must give her time to get used to your tricks.'

Delphine studied Claudie's flushed face with a little smile.

'Take care, *mon chou*,' she warned softly. 'I think the little one may have a few tricks of her own.'

Claudie's colour deepened with the beginnings of temper. There was some kind of game being played between the two of which she was not a part, but of which she seemed to be the butt.

As she searched for the words to retaliate, Delphine picked up her glass and drank thirstily.

'I needed that.' She put down the glass and stood up. 'You have something to show me, Armand? Then show me.' She shot him a teasing glance. 'And since I have no room here, it will have to be yours.'

He laughed. 'Actually, it will be Claudie's room.'

Delphine's brows arched. 'Do you mean they are separate?'

Her eyes sparked mockingly into his in a soundless challenge, which he seemed to ignore.

He said simply, 'But of course.' He turned to Claudie, putting his hand beneath her elbow. 'Lead the way, *chérie*. We are ready to look at your designs.'

He smiled wryly into her apprehensive face. 'Don't be afraid, *ma petite*. Your designs are good. Take my word, Delphine will be enchanted.'

Presented with the drawings, Delphine was suddenly all shrewd businesswoman, and, if her absorbed expression was anything to go by, Armand had been right.

'I like them,' she said at last. She smiled at Armand's satisfied expression and patted his cheek. 'Trust you and that unerring eye, *mon cher*.' To Claudie, she said, 'Have any of these been made up?'

Claudie nodded. 'I've brought some for you to see.'

She opened the wardrobe to show the half-dozen or so ensembles she'd brought and Delphine scrutinised them, her eye alighting eventually on the rainbow gown.

'Oh, but this is delightful,' she cried enthusiastically. 'Such a skilful blend of colours…and the fabric…' She ran her hand over the dress. 'Ah. This one would have to be exclusive.'

'It already is,' Armand broke in, taking it from her and rehanging it in the wardrobe. 'To the designer.'

Claudie stared at him, wide-eyed with surprise. Had he really liked it that much?

Delphine said crossly, 'I thought you were a businessman.'

'A man first,' he said, with a faint smile. 'Claudie will wear it to the show, an original gown seen on the original model. What could be better publicity?'

Delphine's suddenly frowning gaze was on Armand's face. There was a pause as their eyes met and some information seemed to be exchanged.

Then, Delphine turned away with a tight little laugh.

'Some things are priceless, eh, *mon cher*?'

'Precisely.' He closed the wardrobe door with a snap. 'If you've seen enough for now, perhaps we could go down for another drink.' He kissed Delphine's cheek. 'And I expect Michel will have arrived by now.'

She laughed. '*Mais oui*. But don't worry, he won't be alone. A number of the girls are coming on here after rehearsals, to dance a little and unwind.' She cast him a sly little glance. 'It will be a little like old times, *oui*?'

'*Oui*. A little.'

The models had indeed arrived, and already they were clamouring for Armand's attention, urging him on to the small floor to dance. He didn't seem to mind, Claudie thought sourly as he took to the floor with yet another smiling beauty. He was back where he belonged.

They glided by and Claudie had to admit they made a wonderful couple. Tall and dark and statuesque, the girl fitted well against Armand's long frame, anticipating his movements to perfection.

Sitting next to Delphine's husband, who was doing his best to engage her in conversation despite the difficulties of his Parisian French and her poor comprehension, Claudie found her mind wandering. She watched the lithe confidence of Armand's body and felt an unwilling tremor. He could certainly dance and, to her chagrin, she found herself imagining how it would feel to be up there on the floor with him, the movement of his body against hers, swaying to that enticing rhythm.

'Michel,' Delphine cut across her husband's efforts. 'You are boring our guest with your dull talk.' She held out an imperious hand. 'Come! Dance with me and allow Claudie the pleasures of her ringside view.'

There was no doubting the meaning intended in that remark as the model's eyes swung smilingly to Armand and back to Claudie's flushed face.

She said softly as she brushed by, 'But the greater pleasure, *mon chou*, is in participation. *N'est-ce pas*?'

It was humiliating to know her feelings had been so well understood. The only comfort to be gained, Claudie thought miserably, was that Delphine too was probably feeling the same pangs of jealousy.

Her train of thought depressed her. And it didn't help matters when, as one dance finished and another began, Armand came across to Claudie and began drawing her to her feet to dance.

'Thanks, but I'd rather not,' she said tensely, resisting the pull of his hand. To be in his arms in an impersonal way would be impossible, when just the touch of his fingers tugging persistently at hers had her blood pounding in her veins.

'Come, *chérie*. Why resist?' he said a little irritably. 'You are always so concerned with romance. What could be more romantic than Paris, in this setting, on a warm summer evening?'

'Nothing could,' she muttered miserably. 'It would be perfect, if only...'

She stopped, appalled at what her unguarded tongue had been about to reveal.

'Go on, *chérie*,' he encouraged softly, his eyes suddenly intent on her face.

His voice was close to her ear. 'If only...what?'

Claudie squirmed in his arms. Held against him this way, she felt as though her body would burst into flames. Surely he must feel the heat of her fired blood.

'If only there were some real feeling...' she floundered helplessly.

His body, which had begun to sway in time to the music, stilled. 'Do you mean you feel nothing, *chérie*?' He drew her closer, beginning to move again in a persuasive rhythm, one hand against the sensitive curve of her waist, the other holding her fingers prisoner in his palm.

'You *know* what I mean,' she cried angrily.

The small amount of control she was hanging on to so grimly was beginning to melt away. She wanted nothing so much as to wrap her arms about his neck and let herself be carried away by the tide of feelings he was arousing.

He took her hands and placed them on his shoulders.

'Hold me, Claudie,' he commanded.

Feeling her will sapped by his very forcefulness, her fingers crept up to rest against the firm skin of his neck, that neck which she al ady found so irresistible.

His body brushed against hers, a tantalising reminder of other times. Times when she had thought that perhaps... But there could be no going back to that innocence.

He was looking down at her, his dark eyes mysterious in the changing light as they revolved slowly around the tiny floor. Claudie could only look helplessly back at him, wishing desperately that she were anywhere but here... in his arms... where sooner or later she would give herself away.

Perhaps she already had, for he gave a soft laugh and drew her closer so that her breasts were crushed against the hard wall of his chest, lowering his head to lay it against her hair. His breathing had shortened and she could feel it disturbing tendrils of her hair. Even that small evidence of his nearness had an almost devastating affect. It was impossible, suddenly, to go on like this, when every fibre of her being cried out for something more.

And then, as though in answer to her unspoken prayer, the music stopped. The musicians were stepping down off the small dais, signalling the beginning of an intermission. One of the men was setting up some tapes, which emitted a faster, more clamorous sound, and Armand gave a sigh of disgust.

'Just when things were becoming interesting,' he complained, with a teasing light in his eyes.

'Depends on where your interests lie,' Claudie countered, feeling safer as they left the floor.

They arrived back at their table to find it empty. The girls seemed to have dispersed to various partners and Delphine was still dancing.

Claudie was just about to sit down when Armand took her wrist forcefully.

'Don't let's go back to shadow-boxing, Claudie. Take a walk with me along by the river.'

'But the others——' she protested.

'Will find their own amusement,' he said firmly.

Before she could formulate an argument, he'd reached down for her bag and handed it to her.

'Come on. Let's go.'

There was a faint, cooling breeze blowing off the river and the quiet dark gleam of the moon on the water seemed to have a calming effect over Claudie's nerves.

They walked for a long while in a strangely intimate silence, her shoulder leaning against his.

There were snatches of music and laughter from boats that glided by. Few people passed, mainly couples, oblivious to the world about them. Her fears seemed to have faded away into the night.

Armand was holding her hand and she could think of no good reason to snatch it away.

'This is enchanting,' she said, at last, with a little sigh.

In the soft darkness of an archway, he turned her suddenly to face him. 'So are you, *chérie*.'

She knew he would kiss her and made no attempt to draw away. This was the moment she had been waiting for the whole evening. It was madness, she knew, but somehow she didn't care.

His lips held hers sweetly, exploringly, the only urgency in the changing beat of his heart. Her hand was against his chest and she felt the resurgent movement with a sense of wonder.

His tender kiss was exquisite, but made her long, painfully, for more. Without volition, her mouth began its own urgent demand, which he answered, at first with surprise and then with a growing exultation.

Pulling her more tightly into his arms, he kissed her with undisguised passion, his lean hands beginning an arousing exploration, stroking, caressing the sensitive curve of her spine, the gentle swell of her hips, holding her against him with an urgency that had her burning with sensations she had never felt.

She gasped as his hands moved tantalisingly upwards to cup the round softness of her breasts.

He lifted his head at the sound, and his hand slid into the thick tangle of her hair, tilting her head back to look into her face...into her fever-bright eyes.

He murmured, 'Claudie, I...'

The sound of people approaching penetrated her love-hazy mind and, at the same moment, she heard Armand groan.

He put her from him with an irritable gesture. 'I didn't intend this to happen.'

Heat flooded Claudie's already flushed face. Was he trying to say it was her fault? She knew that, if he was, there was some justification.

As the people drew nearer, he grasped her upper arm. 'Let's get out of here.'

Burning with a mixture of humiliation and fury, Claudie allowed him to usher her up stone steps leading to the embankment. Here, lights shone brightly...people moved about...and presumably there was safety in numbers, Claudie thought bitterly.

The grim expression on his face hadn't relaxed, she noted in a sidelong glance, which angered her even more. After all, it had been his suggestion they go walking by the river, not hers.

He put out an impatient hand and a taxi drew swiftly into the kerb. Bundling Claudie into the back, he got in beside her and gave the name of the hotel to the driver.

CHAPTER TEN

BACK at the hotel, Armand paid off the taxi driver and, without a word, led Claudie through Reception and up the wide staircase, his mouth compressed in the familiar grim line.

Feeling miserable beyond words, she just went along with him, wanting only to be alone in her room, where she would probably vent her anger in tears.

Outside of her door, he held out his hand for the key and she fumbled in her bag and brought it out.

Still silent, he opened the door and handed the key back to her.

She kept her eyes averted from his. She didn't want to see the triumph or scorn, or whatever else she might find there. She would have walked silently past him into her room, but he caught her arm, pulling her back towards him.

'Look at me, Claudie,' he commanded.

Unwillingly, she lifted her eyes to his. They were dark and yet gleamed with light so intense that she gasped.

'Now, kiss me,' he ordered.

'Why should I?' Claudie struggled with desire and pride.

'Because you want to. And because I want you to.'

She wanted to resist...with all her will she wanted to...but the magnet of his mouth drew her. She knew the magic it could make against her own and it was irresistible. Reaching up on tiptoe, she placed her lips against his.

He growled, low in his throat, and took his mouth away.

'You can do better than that, *chérie*. By the river, you kissed me with the whole of yourself.'

Claudie stared resentfully up at him. 'That was then,' she retorted unevenly. 'I had rather a lot more wine this evening than I'm used to.'

'Coward.' He touched her cheek. 'Move on, Claudie. There's no way back.'

His words struck a chord somewhere deep inside. She'd known for herself that she'd burned some bridges. It made her squirm to realise he'd known it too.

'Armand,' she said, trying to sound composed, 'where is this leading?'

'To love—if that's what you want. And we both know it is.' His sensuous lips curved and his voice softened in subtle seduction. 'Say my name again, Claudie. You make it sound so good.'

Claudie tried, unsuccessfully, to stifle a tremor of response, and lost control of her heart, which was hammering like a mad thing. 'And if I don't...want...?'

He looked into her eyes for a long moment and then gave a little shrug. 'Just say so.'

That shrug seemed to say it all, she thought, with sudden anger. He was toying with her feelings, punishing her, as he'd been punishing her all evening...probably for her refusal to marry him.

'I don't...want...love,' she asserted, hating the shake in her voice. 'Not your brand, at any rate.'

He frowned darkly. 'Then whose brand? Pascal's?' He gave a short derisive laugh. 'Were you enjoying yourself at the restaurant the other day? It certainly didn't look that way to me.'

'You're so sure of yourself, aren't you?' she blazed. 'It's hard for you to imagine I could prefer Pascal to you.'

'Pascal is still a child. A potentially dangerous child if thwarted. I thought you'd learned that. If not, then I gave you credit for more insight than you have.'

'Thank you. But perhaps I like vulnerable men. Anyway, whom I choose as a lover is my business.'

She wasn't prepared for the fury of his expression, nor for the biting cruelty of his hands digging into the soft flesh of her upper arms.

'You're lying, Claudie,' he gritted, and shook her sharply. 'You can lie with your voice but not with your lips...nor your body.' Without warning, he lifted her bodily into his arms. 'Perhaps I should remind you again of what they have to say when I make love to you.'

Before she had time to utter a protest, he'd elbowed his way into her room, kicking the door shut behind him. Marching across to the bed, he dumped her unceremoniously on to it.

She lay there, speechless with shock, as he began to strip off his clothes, flinging them away from him, across the room.

'And now you, my sweet,' he growled, when he was down to his briefs.

Claudie found her voice as he reached for her. 'Armand, don't. Please don't——'

But he was there on the bed beside her, his lithe body almost naked against her. His mouth closed fiercely on hers, cutting short her entreaty. There was no restraint in him now, no persuasion, no patient waiting for her response. He drove her remorselessly with the searching pressure of his lips, which parted her own and kissed hungrily...deeply...

His leg was across her thighs as he searched for and found the buttons on her blouse. Thrusting the silk aside, he undid the front clasp of her bra, exposing her breasts to the arousing touch of his hands, sending shafts of sensation, piercingly sweet, shooting through her body.

A fever fired Claudie's blood at the warm, sensuous, seeking touch of his mouth against her breasts, his tongue encircling her nipples, making her cry out. Her hands gripped his hair, pulling his mouth back up to hers.

Without lifting his lips from hers, he continued to undress her, his impatient hands seeking hers to help him, which she did with wanton urgency.

Claudie shuddered at the first sweet touch of naked flesh against naked flesh and shivered with delight as his hands moved, unhindered now, against her skin, roaming at will into all the secret places, making her quiver with undreamed of pleasure, driving her towards a crescendo of need that sought relief only in him, making her arch herself against him.

He took her hand, which had been ranging over the muscled sweep of his back, and brought her fingers to his mouth, where he nibbled and caressed each in turn with his tongue, before slowly guiding her hand downwards, over the hard muscle of his chest, the damp heat of his stomach, the crisp curling hairs.

Claudie caught her breath at the contact with that hard core of his desire, and gasped as he moved to enter her, gently at first and then with an urgent demanding rhythm that swept her along on a tide of feeling which burst into ecstasy at the same moment that he found his own fulfilment.

It was dark and Claudie had just wakened from a dream that had her still sighing with pleasure. She'd been sleeping with Armand Delacroix, lying with him in the aftermath of loving such as she had never imagined. Her memory still retained every ecstatic moment of it.

Still basking in the rosy glow of fulfilment, she stirred faintly, not wanting to waken fully. Perhaps, if she kept her eyes closed, her breathing shallow, she could re-capture the dream, sink back into that wonderful place between sleeping and waking, where anything was possible...where just wanting could make it so. She could just reach out and he'd be there.

She'd done it before, many times—conjured him up from the depths of her imagination, into her arms. Only then he'd been a shadowy faceless figure, his loving in-tangible, and her dreams as insubstantial as gossamer. Now, suddenly, she had the power to make him real and she could feel the weight of him in the bed beside her.

She sighed luxuriously and turned on her side, curling her body against the hard-muscled curve of his back, her hands revelling in the smooth firm texture of his skin. She pressed her lips gently against his shoulder, knowing that, if she dared, she could will him to turn...take her back into his arms...love her again...

He stirred, turned and reached out for her and her heartbeat faltered.

'Claudie,' he murmured. '*Chérie* . . .'

Claudie froze with shock. This was no dream...no fantasy. He was here beside her in reality...in her bed. And she *really had* allowed him to make love to her.

'I thought you were sleeping,' he said huskily.

'I was,' Claudie answered. 'I mean...I thought I was...dreaming...'

He gave a soft laugh. 'Then I'm dreaming too.'

He wound his arms about her, his lips touching softly against her forehead, her eyes, the corners of her mouth.

She felt the tremors of her body's reawakening and groaned silently. Come the cold light of morning, how would she face him? How would she face herself?

But, as his kiss deepened, his mouth sensuously demanding all she could give, it ceased to matter. She was in his arms and he wanted her again. And God, how she wanted him!

Her lips answered his fiercely, her hands stroking and caressing, leading wantonly.

He groaned and moved—and he was leaning over her, looking down, his eyes dark pools of desire in the dim light.

She looked back at him, wanting this to go on forever... and felt a surge of something so sweet... so strong... so painful...

'Tell me, *chérie*,' he commanded, 'let me know what you want from me.' His hand, gently brushing the tousled hair from her face, traced a path of fire. 'Say it, Claudie.'

Claudie's heart was about to burst with feelings she had never experienced, never been able to imagine... so bitter-sweet, so urgent, they exploded into words.

'Oh, Armand, I...' She paused. Every part of her was screaming caution... don't go on! 'I think... I've... fallen in love with you.'

The words were so soft... swallowed back by her fear... she was uncertain if they'd been spoken or merely echoed in her head.

He'd pulled her to his side of the bed so that he could look directly down into her face. She looked hesitantly back at him and saw his eyes move away and then close in horror.

He groaned and pulled fiercely back. '*Mon Dieu*! I didn't know.'

Claudie's heart missed a beat—a lurching discomfort. She felt the jolt and cried out.

She'd gone too far...that one step too far...and spoiled it all. How could she have been naïve enough to tell him that she loved him...not to realise he had been waiting for this moment, leading her towards it, step by step?

She turned away, pulling herself from his arms. 'I shouldn't have let it happen.'

She had been warned by enough people. Jacqueline, Pascal, Miranda...even by Armand himself.

'Do you think I don't know that?'

'Oh, I'm sure you do!' she bit back. 'But this wasn't in your scheme of things, was it?'

'Not exactly,' he said grimly. 'Do you think I have no regrets?'

He'd been concerned only with getting her to marry him. Her love would complicate matters considerably when it came to winding up the marriage.

'Perhaps. But not half as much as I regret throwing my love away on a...' She swallowed back a sob.

He reached for her, but she evaded him and he made an impatient little sound. 'It was the first time for you, I know.' His voice was soft. 'But it happens to everyone; you don't have to feel ashamed...'

'I don't.' Claudie's eyes followed his glance to the bedclothes, where the stain of her lost innocence showed stark against the whiteness. She bit her lip. 'At least, not for that. Only for the way I let you lead me on, blindly, like a lamb to the slaughter.'

'Oh, for God's sake!' he cried, with sudden impatience, and sat up. 'Stop it, Claudie. Whether you'll admit it or not, you had a part in this.'

Her colour flared. 'I'm not denying it. But wasn't that all part of your plan in bringing me up here? To seduce me into agreeing to marry you?'

The lines of his face grew hard. 'I'm not into seduction, *chérie*. We both wanted it to happen. At the river...I could have taken you then.'

She flinched. It was obvious he intended to spare her nothing.

'But you preferred your home ground...the privacy and comfort of the hotel,' she shot back at him. 'That's more your style, isn't it? Perhaps I should sign my name in your hotel lovers' log book along with all the others.'

His mouth was a thin, angry line. 'Perhaps you should.'

Claudie's breasts rose and fell with every ragged breath and, as his derisive eyes swept over her, she was suddenly aware that she was naked. Her hands went up involuntarily to cover herself.

'You're too late, Claudie.' He gave a mean little smile. 'By the way, I also keep a score card. Maybe you would like to be included on that also, although discretion will keep me from revealing how far up or down the scale you come.'

Her hand would have made hard contact with his cheek had he not caught her wrist.

Claudie thought about struggling...about beating at him with her other hand to relieve some of her humiliation, but it all seemed suddenly so futile. She slumped back and he released her.

'That's better,' he approved. 'Let's calm down. It's still very early. Maybe we could both do with a little more sleep.'

Claudie sat up again. 'If you think...'

'...that you'd allow me into your bed again,' he finished for her mockingly.

He stood up and began moving about the room, retrieving his discarded clothes.

'Don't worry. I never go where I'm not welcome.'

Staring at his lithe, naked body, the supple strength of him as he bent and straightened, she felt the painful stirrings and became aware of a terrible ache. For good or ill, he'd taught her body how to need him. No fantasy could fulfil her now. She had lost . . . the fantasy and the man . . .

He was heading for the door, his clothes tucked carelessly over his arm.

Claudie stared at him incredulously. 'Aren't you going to put them on?'

'Certainly not. I have my reputation to consider,' he told her with a malicious gleam in his eye. 'Besides, why waste time? The next lucky lady on my list is undoubtedly waiting in my bed.'

He ducked the pillow Claudie flung at him and then stood up again to open the door.

Before he went out, he said, 'Remember, *chérie*, that's how I like it. The next time you want my loving . . . you ask . . . and then wait . . . in my bed.'

Claudie had hoped to avoid Armand Delacroix by coming down late to breakfast, but he was there, engrossed in reading something over his coffee.

He looked up as she sat down beside him and answered her subdued, '*Bonjour*,' with a brisk handshake.

'The tickets for the show,' he said, indicating the papers in his hand.

His eyes flicked over her face, which was pale with faint violet shadows beneath her eyes. She hadn't slept much after he'd left her.

'Delphine left them last night.'

Claudie's spirits plummeted still lower. Perhaps he hadn't been joking after all when he'd said his lover was waiting in his bed.

'That was nice of her,' she murmured, a little caustically. He'd failed in his attempt to seduce her into agreeing to marry him, but he obviously intended going through with the whole charade. 'What time does the show start?' she enquired, in an attempt to display interest.

'Six o'clock. It's exclusive, open to ticket holders only, with a buffet supper afterwards.'

She glanced surreptitiously at her watch. Nine hours to fill before then. How could she endure it?

He saw the gesture and nodded. 'I thought you might like to see a little of Paris beforehand.'

'Yes. I might just wander about a bit later. I did remember to bring my camera.'

He gave one of his short laughs. 'I take it you mean alone?'

Claudie bit her lip. It hurt like mad to deny herself his company, but there was no way she could spend the day with him. After last night it would be too much and, despite his assertion that he would never go where he was not wanted, he knew very well how easy it was for him to make her want him.

'I'm sure you have some...friends...you want to see. I didn't expect to monopolise all of your time.'

To her surprise, he shrugged. 'Very well. If you're sure.'

Claudie thought, sourly, that he hadn't taken much persuading. Perhaps Delphine was still hanging around hoping for her share of his attention. She would be more than delighted to know she could have it all.

'If you take my advice,' he said, 'you'll stick to the tourist areas of the city. It's quite possible to get lost in the alleyways of Paris.'

Claudie bristled. 'I have been to Paris before. I'm not a complete novice.'

'I'm sure not.' His smile was laconic, and she didn't like that cool gleam in his eyes.

'I've done most of the touristy bits, but there are one or two other interesting places I've been promising myself I'd visit, given the opportunity,' she told him, on her dignity. 'I've marked them on a street map.'

She brought the map out and he took it from her, casting an amused eye over the places she'd selected.

'That should keep you out of my way for a while,' he remarked drily.

'Yes.' Claudie frowned at this confirmation of her suspicions that he hadn't wanted to be burdened with her company. 'And you really don't have to spoil your day worrying that I'll get lost.'

'I'll try not to,' he said ironically, ignoring the fiery flash of temper in her eyes. 'There are some people who are interested to meet you this evening, however, and it would be a pity to miss them.'

'I'll be there,' she promised tightly.

'Good.' He put the show tickets into his inside pocket. 'Then I'll leave you to plan your day.' He stood up. 'But, before you leave, I'll just make a note of the hotel telephone number on your map.' He jotted the number on the cover. 'In case you discover you need me after all!'

Watching him walk out of the dining-room, Claudie's blood boiled. Perhaps, given the mood she was in, it was just as well they weren't spending the day together. It would be better if they were at least on speaking terms at the show tonight.

Back in her room, she took out her map and studied it again. Her interest in the Eiffel Tower, Notre Dame and so on had been satisfied on her previous visit, but she wanted to see Montmartre again. She'd start there, she decided, marking it in, and then revisit a wonderful little restaurant on the Left Bank, where the food had tasted unbelievably good.

She highlighted her routes in brightly coloured pencil and folded the map. Her eyes lingered on Armand's handwriting on the cover, wishing idiotically that the number he'd written had instead been a lovers' message. Words she had yearned to hear from him the night before. *'Claudie. Je t'aime.'*

It had rained in the night. Lost in Armand's arms and her dreaming aftermath, she hadn't heard it, but the streets were wet and the trees and flowers glowed like pearls in the pale yellow sunlight.

Despite her earlier misery, Claudie felt the rise of her spirits. It was impossible to be in Paris on a day like this and not want to smile.

The little shops were open in Montmartre and the square was crowded with market stalls selling fruit and vegetables, interspersed with the inevitable artists and their easels. Some wore smocks and stitched leather caps with tiny peaks, attracting a larger share of onlookers to admire, and hopefully buy, their creations.

Artistic ability varied, adding to Claudie's critical absorption, and she had collided with the man before she saw him. He was tall with a thatch of grey hair and ruddy complexion and he apologised in English with an American accent.

'Sorry ma'am—er—*mam'selle.*'

Claudie looked up to answer him, but he'd moved on already, obviously in too much of a hurry to be more than superficially polite. He looked vaguely familiar and she stared after him with a frown. He went into one of the shops, a small, but expensive gallery, with a few select pictures in the carefully dressed window.

Goaded by curiosity, Claudie wound her way around the square until she was standing in front of the shop.

She could see the man inside, talking to another man, and they were both studying a picture placed on an easel.

Claudie gasped with delight as she recognised the painting, a replica, obviously, of one of her favourites by a Dutch artist living in the sixteenth century.

It was while she was eating lunch in the little restaurant on the Left Bank that she suddenly recalled the last time she'd seen the man. He was the American who had been at St Julien and who had accosted Armand and herself in his search for Pascal.

But all thought was pushed from her mind as her eyes settled on a couple eating in a cosy corner.

They were turned away from her, but close enough for them to be unmistakable and for Claudie to hear the man's low voice and the woman's delighted laughter.

Armand and Delphine! Claudie realised with a jolt that had her insides twisting painfully. Armand was holding Delphine's hand and smiling at her with an expression of undeniable admiration.

'Delphine, my angel,' he said in French that came clearly and understandably to Claudie's unwilling ear. 'How long has it been since I told you I adore you?'

Delphine's throaty voice answered, 'Too long.'

The early pale sunshine had faded into a light drizzle. Claudie, in a thin cotton dress, was soon soaked. Not that it mattered; she was already cold through to the bone, chilled by the unexpected proof of her suspicions.

As she wandered the streets unseeingly, an internal battle raged between anger and pointless self-pity.

What had she expected? she asked herself over and over again. He was, as Pascal had said, a womaniser, for whom one woman would never be enough.

Annelise had confirmed that by the stipulation in her will that he should remain faithful to his chosen wife for a year. She had known that, without that motivation, he would never manage it.

Claudie laughed a little hysterically. Having seduced her last night, he hadn't lasted even a day.

But, if she was honest, Claudie would have to admit that Armand had never pretended his interest in her was anything other than selfish.

He'd been quite clearly appalled when she'd admitted she loved him, trying firmly to lay half the blame at her door. It belonged there, God help her, but that didn't ease the pain of knowing that her admission had sent him off, post-haste, to declare his adoration to the woman who really had his love...Delphine Valette.

A situation she might have recognised earlier if she hadn't deliberately buried her head in the sand. Neither of them had made any secret of their association, nor of their continuing feelings for one another.

But why had he pretended an interest in Claudie's designs? There must have been other ways, ways he had used often before, of arranging a clandestine meeting with Delphine.

And, if he loved Delphine, why had he made love to Claudie?

The answer was starkly obvious. To persuade her, at the eleventh hour, to marry him and help him inherit St Julien.

But, if that was the case, why hadn't he followed through on his advantage this morning? Perhaps this evening was destined to be his final attempt. Given her eagerness for his lovemaking last night, he would be feeling sure of an easy conquest. Whatever his reasons, she decided tiredly, it would be impossible to sit beside him at the show tonight, as he watched Delphine on the catwalk, knowing that was where his heart was.

In her present state of mind, she couldn't even bear
the thought of going back to the hotel.

But, if she didn't go back to collect her things, how
was she to get home? She'd brought some money in her
purse, but not enough to make the journey, and her
cheque book was tucked away in her luggage. After a
lot of futile thought, she had, reluctantly, to accept the
fact that she would have to go back to the hotel.

Tired and bedraggled, she trudged over the bridge in
the direction she'd come. After all, she reasoned, if
Armand was there, he could hardly force her to go on
to the show, nor to wait until tomorrow to travel home
with him.

She would shower, change and leave Paris immediately.

With all that sorted out in her mind, she began to feel
more positive. There was bound to be a train available
and she would find transport home somehow from the
station. Better to take one step at a time and deal with
each problem as it arose.

The present problem was how to find her way back
to the Metro. The street into which she'd turned, un-
noticing, was unfamiliar. She walked further along,
searching for the plaque which would give her its name.
Having found it, she delved into her handbag for her
map and cursed herself aloud when she didn't find it.
In her hurry to pay her bill and leave the restaurant, she
must have left the map behind.

Without it, she would have to rely on her memory,
but already she was lost and none of the streets she now
followed were the smallest bit familiar.

She giggled, a little raggedly. What was the matter with
her head? She still had a tongue to ask her way, didn't
she?

There was a man in a dark hat whom she glimpsed
from time to time behind her and who had seemed to

be going her way for some time. She could wait for him to catch up and ask.

But, nearer, a tall, thin man stepped out of a bank building. She stopped him with the lift of her hand.

'*Excusez-moi, monsieur*,' she began politely, '*Je cherche*——'

'Well, well, well! If it isn't *la belle* Claudie!' Pascal's thin face was lit by a beaming smile. 'And lost in the metropolis, if I'm not mistaken.'

Claudie's pale face reddened. 'Yes. I am, as a matter of fact.' She gave a shaky little laugh that was half relief. 'Can you point me in the direction of the Metro?'

Pascal's smile was reassuringly friendly. 'I can do better than that. I can drive you to your hotel if that's where you want to go.'

'Oh, yes. It is,' Claudie cried, relief overcoming her misgivings. 'I can't believe my good fortune in bumping into you.'

'Nor I. It's strange the way fate sometimes takes a hand.'

'Yes, it is.' Claudie had to agree that luck had certainly come her way in the shape of Pascal, however unwelcome a sight he might have been in other circumstances.

'*Voilà*!' A few yards further on, he came to a halt beside his blue sports car and opened the passenger door for Claudie to get in.

She sank into the seat with a sigh of relief. She'd been walking about for what had seemed a long time, but with a bit of luck Armand would still be engrossed with Delphine and she would be able to get in and out of the hotel before he returned.

Pascal got into the driver's seat and started up the engine.

'Where do you wish to go?'

She gave him the name of the hotel.

He nodded and eased out into the traffic, selecting his lane carefully before he spoke again. He cast a curious sidelong glance at her dishevelled appearance.

'I can't help thinking you are in more trouble than having lost your way to the Metro, *ma petite*.' His dark brows rose enquiringly. 'I'm almost tempted to think you're escaping from my dear cousin. It wouldn't be the first time he has driven some poor woman to such despair.'

Claudie bit her lip. She was in no mood now for one of Pascal's diatribes against Armand, however much she might be tempted to agree. 'No. Nothing like that. I just got lost in the rain. What time is it?'

'Ten minutes after four.'

She drew a sharp breath. It was much later than she'd thought. 'And how long will it take before we arrive at the hotel?'

He shrugged. 'Depending on the traffic, perhaps forty or fifty minutes. Are you in a hurry?'

'Yes. No. Oh, I don't know.' Her mind was clouded by confusion and apprehension, almost incapable of rational decision.

Pascal patted her knee comfortingly. 'Well, whatever, you can't do much about it now.'

'No. I suppose not.'

But that didn't stop her fretting. Armand would be sure to be back at the hotel by the time she got there and, in her present state of mind, she just didn't know what she might say to him. If she lost her temper, goodness knew what she might blurt out. Of course, he didn't know she had seen him with Delphine and, if she was to save her pride, she had to make sure he didn't find out. He would be sure to recognise her jealousy.

That was what this was all about, she told herself, with a flash of painful insight. Sheer, agonising jealousy. After having his love, though plainly only physically, she couldn't bear to see him with another woman. Knowing how his kiss felt against her lips . . . the naked touch of his body against her skin . . . she couldn't face the evidence that the same magic was happening with Delphine.

'I adore you,' he'd said, right out there in public, with a look on his face that said much more.

'Pascal,' she said, sounding breathless through her pain. 'After you drop me off, are you going straight home?'

He flashed her a curious glance. 'Home being the estate?'

'Yes.' Claudie's heart leapt at this possible avenue of escape. 'Because, if you are, I wonder if you'd take me with you.'

He smiled slowly. 'If you ask me, *ma belle*, I'll take you to the ends of the earth.'

'Thanks, but I don't think I'm quite up to that.' Claudie's answering smile was weary. 'Just home would be nice.'

The route Pascal was taking seemed to be leading to the ends of the earth, Claudie thought a little anxiously.

On the journey up with Armand, she hadn't noticed there was so much open countryside. But perhaps that was because she'd been more aware of the man than the journey.

Pascal seemed happy. He kept shooting her gleeful looks that somehow made Claudie feel uneasy. He was glad to have had a hand in inconveniencing his cousin again, she knew, but somehow his pleasure appeared to run deeper than that.

They hadn't stopped at the hotel for her things after all. It had seemed more sensible at the time simply to leave for home than to risk the argument that would have been bound to blow up had she arrived to announce she was leaving in company with Pascal.

Armand would be furious and then perhaps worried when she didn't turn up in time for the show. His anxiety had seemed a small retribution for the pain he'd caused her. But, thinking about it more rationally now, the idea seemed far from sensible. Supposing Armand were to alert the police and have her listed as missing or something? How embarrassing that would be to say the least.

'I do think I ought to telephone the hotel and leave a message for Armand,' she suggested tentatively to Pascal, after they'd been travelling for about an hour. 'He's bound to be worried.'

'Let him worry,' Pascal said viciously. 'Pretty soon he'll have a lot more to worry about.'

Claudie sighed, knowing it was useless to argue. It was just as useless to wish the two cousins liked each other better. Annelise's will would ensure that, however things turned out, they would always hate one another.

And when Armand finally found out that she'd gone off deliberately, without even paying him the courtesy of letting him know, he would probably hate her just as much. The thought brought her pain. Not just mental anguish but a deep physical ache for the loving she had experienced so briefly and lost.

'Is this the scenic route?' she asked tiredly, after they'd been travelling for some hours.

Pascal grinned. 'You might say that.'

Claudie frowned. 'I don't recognise any of the places we've passed through; are you sure we haven't got lost?'

'Stop worrying. I've never been more on course.' He touched her knee, squeezing with his thin fingers in a way that made her squirm. 'Why don't you sleep and I'll wake you when we get there?'

Claudie subsided into her seat with a sigh. He was right. There was nothing more she could do, short of having hysterics, and even that was unlikely to produce any desired results.

It was dark when the car finally stopped. Claudie, drifting in and out of an uneasy doze, had lost track of time, but her spirits began to rise as Pascal got out and came around to open the passenger door for her.

'We're here, at last. Home sweet home.'

'Thank goodness.'

Claudie, who had been about to scramble out, was surprised to find herself lifted up into Pascal's arms and carried up a rough path towards a building that was definitely not her house.

As she tensed uneasily, Pascal's grip tightened.

'Where is this place?' Her voice was hoarse with sudden fear. 'You said you'd take me home.'

'This is home,' he reassured her, with a hard laugh. 'That is, my home, now to be yours for a little while.'

He kicked a foot against the front door, which swung back noisily on its hinges, and carried her across the darkened threshold.

'Welcome, *mignonne*!' he said mockingly, kissing her mouth.

Claudie wrenched away angrily. 'Is this some kind of joke, Pascal? Because, if so, I'm in no mood to appreciate it.'

His full lips thinned in a mocking smile. 'Do you mean that in England it is not customary for the groom to kiss the bride after he's carried her across the threshold?'

She felt the trickle of cold perspiration on her brow and knew suddenly that this was no joke.

'Stop playing the fool, Pascal. I'm not your bride.'

'A mere technicality, *ma belle*. This is the perfect place for a honeymoon . . . deep in the heart of the countryside with no neighbours for miles. We can dispense with the piece of paper and the official blessing. Tonight we shall be one in every other sense of the word.'

CHAPTER ELEVEN

PASCAL locked the front door carefully, before going to light the lamps. Claudie stood blinking and looking about.

The house was small, with one large room which served as sitting-room and bedroom, Claudie judged by the dilapidated suite close to the large open fireplace and two ancient beds in opposite corners of the other end of the room.

Another corner was elongated into a recess with a large window, forming a room within a room, which contained two large easels set with canvases and a number of other canvases propped against the walls.

'What do you think of my studio?' he taunted, with a sweeping gesture of his arm about the room.

Play it cool, Claudie advised herself. It's still possible he might come to his senses.

'It's interesting,' she said, trying to sound casual. 'Is this where you normally live?'

'I *exist* here, yes. I wouldn't call it living.' He laughed, an ugly sound. 'But things are about to change. After midnight tonight, it will be too late for Armand to claim the estate by marrying. And tomorrow, everything will be mine.'

Claudie couldn't hide her start of surprise. So, tomorrow was the deadline for Armand to marry. Her stomach clenched. Was it really possible this weekend had been a last-ditch attempt to get her to marry him? If so, when he found her gone, he was going to be very angry indeed. A bubble of laughter that was almost hysterical burst from her lips. Perhaps he'd even had a special licence at the ready and an obliging mayor among the audience at the fashion show, ready and willing to perform the ceremony.

'I'm glad you also find the situation amusing.' He moved forward to grip her arms. 'Because you are going to help me make sure of my inheritance.'

She tried to pull free, but he only tightened his hold.

'You can leave me out of this, Pascal. I've told you before I want no part in what happens between you and Armand.'

'That's a pity, *ma belle*, because, whether you like it or not, you now have the star part.'

He shook her away from him and began pacing the room, his face dark and scowling.

Claudie rubbed at her arms where his fingers had left painful marks and, for the first time, felt fear. Armand had warned her Pascal was dangerous if thwarted, but she hadn't really believed it. Now, she had a terrible feeling she had yet to see the worst of him.

'It's most unlikely Armand will come here. He doesn't even know I was in Paris, so he will not think to look for you with me.' He stopped pacing and stared moodily at her. 'But, to be on the safe side, I intend to make sure that, even if he does come, he will be too late.'

'Wh-what do you mean?' Claudie asked, made breathless by his leering expression and feverish eyes. Was it possible he intended to kill her? Her heart began to race uncomfortably, even as she denied the possibility.

He took hold of her roughly. 'I mean that you and I are going to make each other happy and Cousin Armand very unhappy indeed. By the next time he sees you, you will already belong to me.' He laughed his ugly laugh. 'After which, *ma belle*, he wouldn't want you as a gift.'

'But this is ridiculous, Pascal,' Claudie cried, her voice almost drowned in her head by the thudding of her heart. 'And quite unnecessary. Even if Armand came and begged me, I wouldn't marry him.'

'Who are you trying to fool, Claudie? Me or yourself? You positively drool every time he comes near you. Do you think he hasn't noticed?' He shook his head. 'I can't understand why he didn't press his advantage before this.'

Claudie's face flamed. It was humiliating to have Pascal recognise what she herself hadn't even known until recently, that she was hopelessly in love with Armand Delacroix.

She said, through dry lips, 'You have a wonderful imagination, Pascal. It's a pity you don't put it to better use.'

'Oh, but I do. And I'm sure you'll be the first to applaud my enterprise.' He released one arm and held the other to pull her across the room towards the recess.

He brought her to a halt in front of one of the easels. 'Do you recognise this?'

Claudie's mouth dropped. Of course she recognised it, although she had trouble believing what she saw...an unmistakable early Gauguin.

'Is this...the original?' she asked in astonishment.

Pascal laughed delightedly. 'It could be, couldn't it? But no, it's a little copy I knocked up recently to while away a boring hour or two. Do you like it?'

'I...I think...it's wonderful.' Claudie was almost speechless. 'Perfect, in fact.'

Pascal bowed. '*Merci, mademoiselle. Merci.*' His face glowed with obvious pleasure.

Claudie frowned at him. 'But, with a talent like yours, why are you wasting your time making copies?'

'Ah, well! There are a number of reasons. Firstly, I have imagination, of a practical kind, but, sadly, no originality. And secondly, if you have the right contacts, copies make more money.'

He waved a hand at the Gauguin. 'This was destined to hang in the library of St Julien, in place of the original. But now, it will not. From tomorrow, the original will be mine, along with the rest of the estate, and I shall have no need to steal from myself.'

She shook her head. 'I don't understand.'

He smiled thinly. 'You don't have to, Claudie.' He pulled her to him, his arms like steel bands around her. 'All you have to do is relax and enjoy yourself.'

'Stop it, Pascal. Please.' Claudie tried to keep the panic from her voice. If she could keep control of herself, she might be able to control the situation.

'Oh, come on, sweet innocent!' he jeered. 'You've been playing hot and cold with me long enough, while you've been deciding which horse to gamble on.'

'That's nonsense...'

He put his hand behind her head, drawing her face close to his, where she felt his hot breath on her cheek.

'The race is over and you've backed the winner. Now I claim, in addition to first prize...the second prize also...you!' He grinned triumphantly.

He kissed her fiercely, pressing his mouth against hers so hard her teeth cut into the soft inner flesh, drawing blood, and his fingers dug into her scalp with a force that had her gagging with pain.

Claudie felt the waves of nausea and a rushing sound in her ears.

Oh, God! she prayed. Don't let me faint.

Marshalling all her strength, she pushed at him, sending him staggering back against the wall. Her surprise attack released his hold for a moment and Claudie wriggled free. Then he was reaching for her again and she felt the grip of panic. She started back, crashing into one of the easels, and sending the canvas, with its heavy ornate frame, lurching forward. The corner caught Pascal a blow between the eyes which sounded like a gun retort. He dropped to the floor and lay still.

Claudie's fist flew to her mouth to cover a scream. Oh, my God! If he's dead, what shall I do?

Blood was oozing from a deep gash. Claudie touched it and he gave a faint groan. So, he wasn't dead, only stunned.

She offered silent thanks, but the next moment she was jumping to her feet, as his eyes began to flutter open. She must escape before he came around fully to take his revenge.

She rushed to the door and tried to open it before she remembered Pascal had locked it.

The key, she cried in silent panic. What did he do with the key?

The obvious place was his pocket and she would have to go back. She knelt gingerly beside him to search his clothing, and was just pulling the key from his inside pocket when his hand came up to grab her wrist.

Claudie screamed in fright and tugged with all her strength, trying to break his hold. Then, miraculously, she was free, her fingers as clumsy as thumbs as she fumbled the key into the lock and turned it, pulling the heavy door open with a little cry of relief.

A brief glimpse behind showed her Pascal was lifting himself groggily on to one elbow and rubbing the blood from his eyes with his sleeve. His face was contorted with rage.

It was dark, too dark to see even a step ahead, and Claudie knew it was hopeless to go on. She'd been walking, stumbling, for what seemed miles, guided only by an occasional pinpoint of light in one direction or another. But now, there was nothing but blackness.

The fear and anger had faded, submerged by a growing awareness of her foolish predicament. She hadn't a clue where she was, nor where she was heading. For all she knew, she could have been going around in circles for the past hour.

The roadway had led her to the edge of a wood, but it was impossible to see if it really had petered out or curved away somewhere to the left.

She moved cautiously towards something silhouetted blacker against the murk and found it was a large tree-stump. She sat down on it with a weary sigh. There was little point in going on further. Earlier, her concern had been that Pascal would recover enough to give chase, but now it seemed unlikely he would catch up with her, at least not until early light. She might just as well rest until then. The tree-stump was large and round and smooth where the saw had cut cleanly. A far safer bet for a bed than the ground, which would be crawling with insects and possibly even snakes, she thought with a shudder.

The night was warm and Claudie's hair was damp with sweat. She took off her jacket and rolled it up for a pillow. Not exactly a luxury Paris hotel, she told herself with an attempt at humour, but better than a night under Pascal's inhospitable roof.

Lying down, she could see that the night wasn't completely dark. The moon wasn't visible, but tiny pinpoints of light that must have been stars showed through the leafy branches overhead, which swayed in a gentle breeze.

Watching the movement helped take her mind off the fact that she had run away from two men in one day. One man would probably be hopping mad, the other demented, and she wished fervently that she might never have to see either of them again.

She seemed to have been sleeping only for seconds, when the light woke her. It shone strongly into her eyes, almost blinding her as she sat up with a groan. It took a few seconds for her to realise that she was looking, not at the dawn, but almost directly into the headlights of a car.

Her first instinct was to jump up and wave her arms for attention, but that was before she thought of Pascal. He would undoubtedly be searching for her and, as much as she might try to make a joke of the situation, there would be nothing funny about finding herself again in his clutches.

She jumped off the tree-stump and began to run, away from the light, knowing it shone on her like a spotlight. Turning, she plunged into the wood, lurching through the undergrowth like a blind man.

'Claudie. Stop.'

Claudie's heart beat almost to bursting point. Oh, God! The voice was close.

'Don't be a fool! Stop!'

He was gaining on her. She could hear him crashing through the brush close behind her and began to whimper as her strength ebbed.

She screamed as two hands grabbed her from behind and swung her around.

'You little fool! What on earth's got into you?'

'Armand?' she gasped. 'Is it really you?'

'Who else would be chasing an idiot girl through a wood in the dead of night?' There was relief as well as warmth in his voice.

Claudie flung herself at him, almost knocking him over in her haste to find the safety of his arms.

'Thank God you found me!' She swallowed back a sob. 'I thought you never would.'

His arms, wrapped tightly around her, felt like a haven from which she never wanted to emerge.

'So did I for a while. But we'll talk about that later.' He kissed her in a way that had her heart singing, then lifted her and carried her to the car. 'We're going back to the hotel and you can get some sleep on the way. After that, we'll talk.'

'How did you know where to find me?' Claudie still had difficulty believing her luck.

She was sitting in bed, with a breakfast tray across her knees, brought, to her surprise, by Armand. He'd arranged it carefully, solemnly tucking her napkin into the neck of her nightgown, before seating himself on the edge of her bed.

He said, 'You're not going to like the answer to that one.'

'Never mind. Tell me.' She poured coffee into a cup and sipped it appreciatively.

'I had someone keep an eye on you while you were sightseeing, just to be on the safe side and——'

'You did what?' Claudie spluttered in outrage, setting her cup rattling in its saucer.

He lifted broad shoulders in a shrug. 'I couldn't take a chance on you getting lost.'

'I wasn't lost,' she said indignantly. 'Just a little off course. I'd have got there eventually...if I hadn't bumped into Pascal.'

He gave a short laugh. 'Bumping into Pascal was probably no accident. I've thought for some time he might try to get at me through you, which was another reason why I took the precaution of having a man look after you. And if he hadn't followed Pascal's car and rung me to let me know where he'd taken you, goodness knows what might have happened.'

Claudie shuddered. She knew exactly what would have happened. Pascal had been graphic in his intentions. Rape, in the hope that it would turn Armand off any ideas he might have of last-minute marriage.

She frowned. 'How did you know Pascal was in Paris? He didn't seem to think you did.'

'I have Miranda Belling to thank for that piece of information. She rang me at the hotel to tell me that she had *inadvertently* let Pascal know our plans for the weekend and she feared he might be planning something unpleasant.'

Claudie frowned. 'That's a surprise, since she was decidedly unfriendly herself just before we left.'

He gave a short laugh. 'Letting Pascal know where you were was more than unfriendly. It was a big mistake and she knew it. Once she'd had time to think, she realised what I would do if anything serious happened to you.'

'Armand,' Claudie began tentatively. 'Did you . . . ask her to marry you?'

He shot her an astonished look. 'Miranda Belling? *Mon Dieu*! Whatever gave you that idea?'

'Well, practically every time I saw you, you seemed to be with her.'

'She was my secretary, for heaven's sake,' he said irritably.

Claudie bit her lip. 'Only in working hours. There were a lot more hours left, with you two together in that big house.'

Until that moment, she hadn't actually acknowledged that thought, but it had obviously been in her mind.

'Don't be ridiculous,' he said. He sat on the bed and coiled a tress of her hair about his finger.

'But you went off with her at the feast,' she insisted, wishing he'd sit somewhere else ... somewhere a little further away, so that she could think clearly. 'You were gone a long time.'

'I know,' he said, releasing her hair with a sigh. 'And I'm sorry. But time was of the essence. She'd come because she'd followed Pascal and had seen him hide one of the paintings from the house in the disused barn. I was hoping to catch him there, but he'd gone.'

'I see.' Claudie frowned. 'What exactly was he doing with the paintings? He said something about not needing now to steal from himself.'

He made a harsh sound. 'He's been stealing from the house, for some time apparently... original paintings which he sold after replacing them with his own replicas.'

'Now I understand what he meant by copies making more money than his own originals.' Claudie shook her head. 'How did you find out?'

He grimaced. 'Miranda knew for some time. She'd seen the furtive swappings, but she said nothing until after Annelise died, when she finally decided to tell.'

'Why did she then?' Claudie asked, still curious, though a little less puzzled.

He smiled. 'She knew the contents of the will. Perhaps she hoped my gratitude for her *loyalty* might prompt me into a proposal of marriage.'

'I thought so too,' Claudie admitted. 'I didn't know about the paintings, of course, but when I turned you down Miranda seemed the next logical choice. After all, there weren't all that many *local* girls for you to choose from, and you did need to marry in a hurry.' She bent her head.

He gave a deep sigh and gripped her arms none too gently.

'*Chérie*, I didn't *need* to marry...you or anyone else. I make a very good living without it. I've never needed Annelise to subsidise my income. If she'd cut me off without a penny, it wouldn't have made much difference to my lifestyle, only to my heart. I've always loved St Julien, where I spent the happiest years of my life.'

'How could Annelise even dream of taking it away from you?'

'She didn't. She knew as well as I did that, French property law being what it is, it would be very easy to overthrow her will. Unlike Pascal, I'm of the Delacroix blood. As a legally adopted son, even having failed to meet the stipulations, my claim would be certain to take precedence.'

Claudie sighed irritably. 'Then why did she make the stipulation that you marry as a condition to you inheriting St Julien?'

He laughed. 'Annelise at her most stubborn... attempting to have the last word. She set the scene, with both of us on the spot, and hoped nature would do the rest.'

She looked away, her face faintly flushed. 'And the one about being faithful?'

'Was a warning, I believe.' His dark eyes gleamed wickedly down at her. 'That if I did have the luck to marry her precious god-daughter, I would have to change my wicked ways.'

Claudie said, with a little quake in her voice, 'And could you? I mean...change your ways?'

'Of course. They were never as wicked as she feared.'

'But, as you say, you get St Julien...without having to change a thing.' Her fingers plucked absently at the edge of the bedcover. 'You're free to marry who you like when you like.'

He grinned. 'Precisely. Annelise will be furious, but that's where I have the last word after all.' He stood up. 'Now perhaps I should leave you to finish your breakfast and rest.'

Claudie's heart was unaccountably heavy. 'Shall we be leaving for home today?'

'Possibly. I have a number of things to see to before then.'

Like some unfinished business with Delphine, Claudie thought miserably.

'How was the fashion show?' she asked a little flatly.

'It wasn't,' he said crisply. 'Not from my point of view anyway. I was too busy charging about the countryside in search of a mule-headed girl.'

'I'm sorry.' Claudie coloured. 'I might not have got lost...or gone off with Pascal...if I hadn't seen you with...'

'Delphine at the restaurant?' He finished her sentence with a question.

'Yes,' she admitted in a crushed voice. 'How did you know? Your detective?' This last on a derisive note.

'No. I found your map, with my scrawl on the cover. You dropped it on your way out.' He scrutinised her flushed face. 'Why did you rush off like that? Why didn't you come across and say hello?'

'Because I...' She shook her head, lowering her giveaway eyes from his. 'I didn't want to intrude.'

His dark brows rose. 'On what?'

'Your conversation with Delphine. It seemed...rather personal.'

'Did it?' He frowned. 'I don't remember...'

Before she could stop herself, Claudie had blurted it out.

'Can you really forget that quickly, having told a woman you adore her?'

He stared blankly for a moment and then a slow smile spread across his face. 'That romantic mind of yours, *chérie*. You see already how it makes complications.'

Claudie's temper began to rise, an outlet for her misery.

'I see nothing complicated about the fact that you're in love with Delphine Valette.' Her tray rattled in her suddenly trembling hands.

'Don't you?' He took the tray and put it on a side-table, coming back to sit on the bed beside her. 'Wouldn't you call a husband a complication?'

'*I* would,' she shot back at him, made nervous by his nearness and the strange expression in his dark eyes. 'But we're not concerned with my opinions.'

'Wrong,' he said drily. 'I'm very concerned, *chérie*. Tell me . . . how do you feel about the fact that I might be in love with Delphine?'

She stared at him resentfully. 'It's not my business, is it?'

There were strange, disconcerting lights dancing in his eyes. 'Isn't it? Even though I made love to you?'

'Of course not. I have no claim over you. You can please yourself.'

'Ah!' He gave her a slow smile, which did weird and wonderful things to her insides. 'If I were to please myself, then I would take you in my arms to kiss some awareness into that blind heart of yours.'

'Why should you want to do that?' Despite her confusion, Claudie felt a surge of hope.

'Why do you think?'

She gave a cry of frustration. 'Don't ask questions. Answer them!'

'Very well.' He took her face in his hands and kissed her mouth with the gentlest of pressure, that sent a shiver of delight rippling through her. After a while, he lifted his head. 'Does that answer your question, *chérie*?'

'I think so,' she said breathlessly. 'I'm not sure.'

He grinned. 'Perhaps I should be more explicit.'

He made to take her in his arms, but she held him off.

'Armand, how much *do* you adore Delphine?'

He said solemnly, 'As much as any man would, when she had just come up with an idea that would benefit very much the career of the woman he loved.'

Claudie's gaze widened on his. She said tentatively, 'Are you saying you love me?'

He folded his arms about her and this time she didn't resist.

'I am saying, sweet idiot, that I loved you almost from the first moment I set eyes on you. I fought it only because I couldn't rid myself of the suspicion you might have been in league with Annelise. And I couldn't let two women win in a plot to organise my life, however well intentioned.'

As his lips sought hers, she still fought him, though her heart swelled with a feeling that could only be joy, and yet...

'Armand, if you loved me, why did you react so strangely when I told you I loved you?'

He looked down at her, with a little frown between his brows. 'I don't understand.'

She shook her head in dismay. 'You must remember. When we were making love...again...in the morning. I told you I was in love with you and you...seemed more concerned about my lost...'

'Ah!' His eyes lit with sudden understanding. He said softly, 'Forgive me that misunderstanding, *chérie*. And tell me again that you love me.'

Shyly, she looked up at him, but the words wouldn't come.

He kissed her, slowly, deeply, until she was breathless.

'Tell me now,' he whispered, as he finally lifted his mouth from hers.

'Oh, Armand. I love you.'

'And I love you, *chérie*.'

He kissed her again, brushing his mouth against her lips, her eyes, her temples, her throat.

Claudie's head swam, but there was one last little barrier to be surmounted.

'Armand.' Her voice was slow and husky. 'I really would prefer to manage my own career.'

He moved back in astonishment.

'And I thought you were the romantic one.' He sighed and put her from him to look down into her face. 'OK,' he said at last. 'If that's what you want.'

She nodded. 'It's *one* of the things I want.' Pulling back the covers, she got out of bed.

'Claudie,' he said, on a heavy sigh, 'where are you going now?'

She touched his cheek. 'Somewhere where, hopefully, I'll get the rest of what I want.' Crossing the room, she opened the door on to the landing. 'Is your room open?'

'I think so. Why?'

She smiled demurely. 'If you'll give me a minute before coming in, you'll find out.'

Slipping out of the room, she went into his, discarding her nightgown before getting into his bed.

He was there, standing in the doorway, his eyes drinking in the naked beauty of her, a questioning smile on his lips.

'Well, Armand?' she said softly. 'I'm waiting. Just the way you like it.'

He growled, deep in his throat. 'For shame, Claudie.'

She shook her head. 'No shame, Armand. I love you.'

In a couple of strides he crossed the room, pulling off his clothes as he went.

She sighed and lay back, her arms reaching out as he came to her, gasping as his mouth claimed hers in a kiss that scorched her through and his hands began an arousing exploration. It was some time before she could think clearly again.

She lay in his arms, happy and replete, but with the questions still buzzing around in her head.

'Armand, do you really believe Annelise meant you to marry me?'

He groaned and turned so that he could look into her face. 'Yes. I do.'

'Why do you suppose she wanted that?'

'Because she wanted us both to be happy and obviously thought we'd make an ideal couple.'

'Whatever made her think that?' she asked wickedly.

'I can't imagine.' His face was expressionless.

She sighed. 'I really didn't know, you know.'

'I know,' he said patiently. 'Annelise was astute. She understood you well enough to realise that if you had any idea of her plans you would work stubbornly against them.'

'Yes. I suppose she did,' Claudie admitted fairly. 'So she left me the house and hoped for the best.' She sighed. 'Oh, well. It was worth a try... even if she failed.'

'Failed?' He frowned. 'Failed in what?'

'In getting us married off, of course.'

He scowled down at her. 'Do you mean you *still* refuse to marry me?'

She met his gaze innocently. 'I can hardly refuse... or accept... until I've been asked.'

'Claudie Drew! You wicked lady,' he growled and nibbled her ear in retribution, before whispering, 'Well? Will you marry me?'

She sighed. 'Do you think you'll manage to stay faithful for a year?'

'Claudie!' This time, the growl was a warning.

'Yes, please,' she said quickly.

He kissed her deeply and satisfyingly, before tucking her head into the hollow of his shoulder.

From the warmth of his embrace, she asked him, 'Armand, how long *will* you stay faithful?'

'To inherit *your* heart?' He tipped her chin to look into her eyes. 'Forever.'

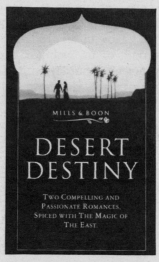
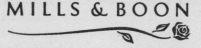

Next Month's Romances

Each month you can choose from a wide variety of romance with Mills & Boon. Below are the new titles to look out for next month, why not ask either Mills & Boon Reader Service or your Newsagent to reserve you a copy of the titles you want to buy – just tick the titles you would like and either post to Reader Service or take it to any Newsagent and ask them to order your books.

Please save me the following titles:	Please tick	✓
NO RISKS, NO PRIZES	Emma Darcy	
ANGEL OF DARKNESS	Lynne Graham	
BRITTLE BONDAGE	Anne Mather	
SENSE OF DESTINY	Patricia Wilson	
THE SUN AT MIDNIGHT	Sandra Field	
DUEL IN THE SUN	Sally Wentworth	
MYTHS OF THE MOON	Rosalie Ash	
MORE THAN LOVERS	Natalie Fox	
LEONIE'S LUCK	Emma Goldrick	
WILD INJUSTICE	Margaret Mayo	
A MAGICAL AFFAIR	Victoria Gordon	
SPANISH NIGHTS	Jennifer Taylor	
FORSAKING ALL REASON	Jenny Cartwright	
SECRET SURRENDER	Laura Martin	
SHADOWS OF YESTERDAY	Cathy Williams	
BOTH OF THEM	Rebecca Winters	

If you would like to order these books in addition to your regular subscription from Mills & Boon Reader Service please send £1.90 per title to: Mills & Boon Reader Service, Freepost, P.O. Box 236, Croydon, Surrey, CR9 9EL, quote your Subscriber No:................................... (if applicable) and complete the name and address details below. Alternatively, these books are available from many local Newsagents including W H Smith, J Menzies, Martins and other paperback stockists from 9 September 1994.

Name:..

Address:...

....Post Code:...........................

To Retailer: If you would like to stock M&B books please contact your regular book/magazine wholesaler for details.

You may be mailed with offers from other reputable companies as a result of this application. If you would rather not take advantage of these opportunities please tick box. ☐

Barbara

DELINSKY

A COLLECTION

New York Times bestselling author Barbara Delinsky has created three wonderful love stories featuring the charming and irrepressible matchmaker, Victoria Lesser. Worldwide are proud to bring back these delightful romances — together for the first time, they are published in one beautiful volume this September.

THE REAL THING
TWELVE ACROSS
A SINGLE ROSE

Available from September   Priced £4.99

W❂RLDWIDE

Available from WH Smith, John Menzies, Volume One, Forbuoys, Martins, Woolworths, Tesco, Asda, Safeway and other paperback stockists.

Win a Year's Supply of romances
ABSOLUTELY FREE!

YES! you could win a whole year's supply of Mills & Boon romances by playing the Treasure Trail Game. Its simple! - there are seven separate items of treasure hidden on the island, follow the instructions for each and when you arrive at the final square, work out their grid positions, (i.e **D4**) and fill in the grid reference boxes.

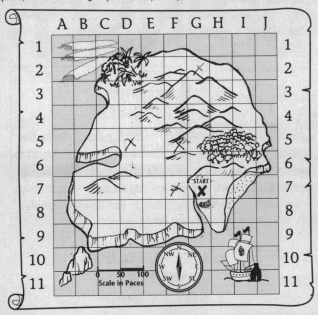

From the start, walk 250 paces to the **North**.

GRID REFERENCE

| G | 2 |

Now turn **West** and walk 150 paces.

GRID REFERENCE

| D | 2 |

From this position walk 150 paces **South**.

GRID REFERENCE

| D | 5 |

Now take 100 paces **East**.

GRID REFERENCE

| F | 5 |

Then 100 **South**.

GRID REFERENCE

| F | 7 |

And finally 50 paces **East**.

GRID REFERENCE

| G | 7 |

Please turn over for entry details

SEND YOUR ENTRY
NOW!

The first five correct entries picked out of the bag after the closing date will each win one year's supply of Mills & Boon romances (six books every month for twelve months - worth over £90). What could be easier?

Don't forget to enter your name and address in the space below then put this page in an envelope and post it today (you don't need a stamp).

Competition closes 28th Feb '95.

TREASURE TRAIL Competition
FREEPOST
P.O. Box 236
Croydon
Surrey CR9 9EL

Are you a Reader Service subscriber?   Yes ☐   No ☐

Ms/Mrs/Miss/Mr _____ COMTT

Address _____

_____

_____

_____ Postcode _____

Signature _____

One application per household. Offer valid only in U.K. and Eire. You may be mailed with offers from other reputable companies as a result of this application. Please tick box if you would prefer not to receive such offers. ☐